D1636188

Alias Dix Ryder

Alias Dix Ryder

William Colt MacDonald

Thorndike Press • Chivers Press
Thorndike, Maine USA   Bath, England

This Large Print edition is published by Thorndike Press, USA and by Chivers Press, England.

Published in 1999 in the U.S. by arrangement with Golden West Literary Agency.

Published in 1999 in the U.K. by arrangement with Golden West Literary Agency.

U.S.   Hardcover   0-7862-2193-3   (Western Series Edition)
U.K.   Hardcover   0-7540-3973-0   (Chivers Large Print)
U.K.   Softcover   0-7540-3974-9   (Camden Large Print)

The text of this Large Print edition is unabridged.
Other aspects of the book may vary from the original edition.

Set in 16 pt. Plantin.

Printed in the United States on permanent paper.

British Library Cataloguing-in-Publication Data available

Library of Congress Cataloging-in-Publication Data

MacDonald, William Colt, 1891–1968.
    Alias Dix Ryder / William Colt MacDonald.
        p. (large print) cm.
    ISBN 0-7862-2193-3 (lg. print : hc : alk. paper)
    1. Large type books. I. Title.
[PS3525.A2122A79   1999]
813'.52—dc21   99-41714

Alias Dix Ryder

Chapter I

Santone Austin had taken four days to make his way up from Tucson, after riding out of Tombstone. At times he had pushed the roan gelding hard; at others he had just loafed along the way, sleeping in the open when the day was done, or, when an outfit was near, getting his bait and shut-eye where convenient. On two occasions he had been offered jobs which were declined. Probing questions from the curious he had just laughed off, explaining he was just riding through to see the country, while admitting openly that Texas was his home originally. As to his reason for leaving Texas, he never explained, and there was that in Santone Austin's manner which precluded too searching questions.

That he was "cow-country stuff," no one could doubt. Santone Austin was somewhere in the vicinity of thirty years with dark hair — one lock of which was always slipping down on his forehead when his weather-worn sombrero was removed — steely-gray eyes, good features and a lean, stubborn jaw. In a time and country when many men grew beards, or sported mustaches, he was cleanshaven. Somewhere around six feet tall with broad shoulders and deep chest, he was lean-hipped.

A coat and burlap sack were rolled behind his saddle cantle. His overalls — bibless — were well-worn but clean, as was his woolen shirt; his high-heeled riding boots somewhat scuffed. A wide cartridge belt hung low at one hip and supported a scarred holster holding a walnut-butted, single-action Colt's forty-four caliber six-shooter. Every ounce of man and equipment appeared to be in full commission.

Now, as the trail he was following carried him toward the cow-town of Arboledo, he began to see clumps of cottonwoods, and farther off, against a background of the Sangriento Mountains, he spied occasional bunches of white-face cows eating their way through the lush, waving grass.

"Looks like good grazing lands hereabouts," he mused. "Heaps different than down south way where desert country looks always ready to take over, and this is some change from all that up-and-down rocky scenery. Arboledo. Hmm-m-m. Let's see" — searching his memory for the translation from Spanish — "if I'm not mistaken, the word means woodland, or something to do with trees. Likely there was a regular clump hereabouts until Arboledo took over. And there's always mesquite wherever I ride, seems like. And cactus." He squinted toward the distant Sangriento Mountains. "Looks like there'd be some piñon growing on those slopes."

He nudged the roan gelding with his spurs, and the animal quickened pace along the trail. He pushed down across a dry-wash, lined sparsely on either side with cottonwoods, the horse picking its way carefully over the rock-cluttered way, and climbed up on the opposite side. Once more waving grass bordered the trail, with an occasional clump of opuntia cactus or mesquite breaking the monotony of view. A few pines began to appear and more cottonwoods, then a scattering of adobe shacks as he neared Arboledo. Overhead a few fleecy clouds played tag against the sapphire sky.

When he entered the main street, the town appeared much like any other cowtown. An unpaved thoroughfare, probably muddy in winter, but at present wagon-rutted and hoof-chopped, dusty, with a few chickens picking in the dust under the torrid sun. Glancing down one cross street, Santone Austin saw a railroad depot and freight shack, beyond which were shipping pens, awaiting the fall shipment of beef animals.

There were the usual buildings along the main street — false-fronted buildings and smaller adobe structures. Austin walked the roan along the thoroughfare until the buildings began to thin out again. He noticed several men look sharply in his direction, and one or two appeared about to hail him.

Austin mused, "A stranger in this town certainly creates a mite of interest. Anyway, I haven't yet seen anybody who looks familiar."

He turned the pony back toward the way from which he'd come, seeing three saloons, two general stores, a tiny post office, a couple of barber shops, a bank and various other buildings of commercial enterprise. A livery stable and a hotel was what he sought at present, but a cold beer was among his immediate needs. Men still eyed him sharply as he rode past. There were quite a few on the plank sidewalks or loitering in the shadows between buildings or on porches, many of whom were Mexicans. Cowponies stood patiently at hitch-racks. Now and then a rider loped past, kicking up clouds of dust at his rear. One loping rider looked as though about to draw rein and speak to Austin, but apparently changed his mind and drove on. Twisting in his saddle, Austin looked around and saw the rider glancing back at him.

"Damn funny situation when a stranger in town stirs up so much curiosity," Austin muttered. "I sure hope I don't look like some hombre on a reward bill in the sheriff's office. I've seen enough hot lead coming my way, in my time. All's I want now is peace and quiet. Maybe it might be smart to push on after I've had a cold beer and wetted down the pony's gullet."

He heard a voice call "Hey, Dix!"

He glanced toward the sidewalk and saw a man in civilian clothing looking his way. Austin thought, "He must be calling to somebody else," so he paid no attention. "Anyway, I'm not Dix."

The man who had called the greeting was standing stockstill at the edge of the sidewalk, a puzzled look on his bewhiskered features. He waved again in Austin's direction. Austin smiled slightly and pulled the roan back toward the center of the road. "Looks like," he cogitated, "that feller takes me for somebody else. I've never been here before, or even in Arizona Territory before. I got a good look at the man, and I'm fair certain I never knew him back Texas way."

Kicking the sweat-and-alkali streaked pony in the ribs with his heels, he pushed on, turning toward the sidewalk in the next block, toward a building bearing a wide sign which proclaimed it to be the Arboledo Saloon. Here he drew rein and dismounted at a watering trough and while the horse was quenching its thirst, he loosened the saddle cinch. While Austin was waiting for the roan to finish drinking, he glanced toward the saloon porch where half a dozen men were loafing, the backs of their wooden chairs tilted against the front wall of adobe. Two of the men were Mexicans who gave him a cheerful smile and nodding of sombreroed heads. Austin returned their nods, before noticing he was getting only scowls from the others, two of whom left their chairs and hurried off down the street. The two who remained pretended to take no further notice of Austin, though their scowls deepened.

Austin left the hitch-rack and stepped to the porch. The Mexicans were still smiling, something almost of a welcome in their manners.

"*Buenas tardes, señores,*" Austin smiled at the Mexicans. "Or 'Howdy,' just as you like."

"*Buenas tardes,* Señor Dix," the two spoke in unison. One of them started to add, "It is good to see you —" but broke off abruptly as one of the scowling men snarled something in his direction, and fell into silence.

Austin didn't catch what the scowling man had said, but judged he was correcting the Mexican for greeting him as Dix Somebody-or-Other. He didn't like the tone of the man's voice and hesitated a moment, then deciding it was none of his business what passed between these strangers, passed on into the saloon, the bat-wing doors swinging at his back as he pushed through.

It was cool and dim within the saloon and Austin paused a moment to adjust his vision after the sun-glare of the street. There was only one man standing at the bar, a bottle and a glass before him, just nursing along his drink. A rather hard-looking individual he was, too. The weighty bartender, a white apron tied about his bulging middle, stood with his

13

fat back to the bar, stacking some clean glasses on the back-bar.

Austin's glance ran over the place. It seemed orderly enough, bottles and glasses held a certain polish. The bar was clean and, apparently, had a coat of varnish recently. It ran along one side of the room; the remainder of the swept floor had space enough for four wooden square tables, each with wooden chairs accompanying. A few pictures, cut from a pink-sheeted magazine of that day, adorned the walls, showing prize fighters, race horses, and burlesque actresses. The back-bar mirror was free of flyspecks, contrary to so many bar mirrors Austin was accustomed to seeing. There was a doorway at the back of the saloon, the door now standing open, allowing such breeze as there was to blow through.

Santone Austin started toward the bar, his spurs jangling on the wooden floor planks. He removed his sombrero and with a bandanna handkerchief dabbed at his moist forehead. At the sound of the spur rowels, the lone customer at the bar half turned around, glancing idly at Austin, then swung back to his drink. Abruptly, something seemed to electrify him, and he turned suddenly for another look at Austin.

For a second his jaw dropped, his eyes bulged, he seemed to turn ashen. He raised one hand to brush across his eyes, as though to shut out some unwelcome sight. He gulped like a fish out of water as he stared at Austin, then found his voice:

"My Gawd," he quavered. "I — I — no! No!" The last syllable was almost like the frightened yelp of some cur, as he left the bar, knocking over his drink in his haste and fled through the open door at the back of the saloon.

Austin frowned. Now what was going on? Everything in this town seemed sort of haywire, somehow.

The fat bartender had turned at the sound of the frightened yelp and looked in amazement toward the door through which his customer had scrambled.

"Hey, Faxon!" he yelled. "Wottenhell's got into you?"

But Faxon was moving too fast to answer, and had already disappeared from sight.

"Hey, you, Faxon!" the barkeep shouted exasperatedly, "come back and pay up for that last drink." He swore angrily. "That cheap chiselin' bastard!" He started to mop up Faxon's spilled drink.

Austin had replaced his sombrero by

now as he continued his walk toward the bar. He chuckled. "He acted like a hen-pecked husband trying to evade his wife. Still I didn't hear any female voice out front —"

"Wife?" The barkeep was still staring toward the open rear door. "Ain't no woman, decent or otherwise, would marry up with that scum," he finished disdain-fully. Now he swung his ponderous belly around as Austin halted before the bar. Then his eyes bulged. His heavy form banged against the back-bar as he staggered back. The blood seemed to leave his face. Then he regained his poise and leaning across the bar stared closely at Austin.

"Sufferin' rattlers!" he exclaimed. "It just can't be, but for a moment I — I thought —"

Austin smiled, saying dryly, "You two must have rehearsed that henpecked act —"

"Ain't — ain't got no wife," the barkeep stuttered.

"Sure, 'Ain't no woman — decent or otherwise . . . ,' " Austin quoted the bar-keep — but the barkeep's next words stopped him short.

"Dix! Dix!" the fat man gurgled. "You are back, back from the dead!"

Chapter II

Now it was Santone Austin's turn to stare blankly. "What in the devil you talking about? Do I look like I'd been dead? My name is certainly not Dix —"

The fat bartender chuckled. "Come down off'n that hawss," he protested. "There's a limit to how long you should pull my leg. For a minute when I first laid eyes on you, I figured I'd seen a ghost. Then when you took me up, repeatin' my own words, y'know, about 'no woman, decent or otherwise,' I was certain 'twas you. That's just like you used to do. Where in Gawd's name you been, Dix? They said you was dead."

"Who said I was dead?"

"Why — why, everybody, includin' your wife. She got proof —"

"My wife — ?" Austin exclaimed. He laughed scornfully. "Next you'll be claiming I'm henpecked too. This Arboledo town is sure full of crack-brained ideas. Let's cut it out, barkeep. My throat's full of sand. You can explain after I've had a long drink of water and a cold beer."

The bartender shrugged somewhat disappointedly. "Dam'd if I know why you want to keep on hurrahin' me — an old friend like me. But it's up to you, Dix."

He set out a bottle of beer and a tall tumbler of water. Austin emptied the water glass and then refilled it with beer and took two deep gulps. Thirst slacked, he lifted Durham and brown papers from a shirt pocket, twisted a cigarette and lighted it. Gray and blue smoke drifted lazily through the room. All the time the barkeep was eyeing him in puzzled fashion.

Austin finished the bottle of beer, commenting, "You keep good suds, anyway. It's good to find San 'Tonio beer so far from Texas."

"Yep, that's the beer that made Milwaukee jealous." The bartender set out another bottle, employed a screwdriver-like opener to lift out the small metal cup-stopper. "This one is on the house."

"Thanks." Austin refilled the glass, took a sip and smiled at the fat man. "So you thought I was dead."

"How could folks think otherwise," came the earnest reply.

"Do I look dead?" Austin smiled.

Dumbly, the barkeep shook his head.

"Can't say you do," he admitted uncertainly. "But, look here, Dix, where in time you been — ?"

Austin broke in, "There you go with that Dix name again. You're mighty mistaken, man. My name's not Dix — it's Austin, Santone Austin. Do you think you can remember that?"

"I'll remember what you said. *Hmmm.* Santone Austin, eh? Sounds like a made-up name to me."

Austin laughed. "Y'know, I've often thought that myself. But there it is. Back home in Texas, nobody ever calls me anything else."

"You mean to say, you still maintain" — unbelievingly — "that you ain't Dix Ryder?"

"Get it straight," Austin said somewhat testily, "I'm Santone Austin, formerly of Texas. Now I'm sort of footloose, just — well, it doesn't make any difference what I'm doing now."

"I'll be damned," the fat man ejaculated fervently, "if you ain't the spittin' image of Dix Ryder, I'm a purple pack-mule."

Austin grinned. "Anyway, I'd sure hate to see you turn purple, and you look a mite weighty to be a pack-mule."

"Ain't it a fact? My name's Frank Sullivan, but everybody calls me Porky around Arboledo."

Austin said dryly, "I'd never guess the reason."

The fat man ran one hand over his slicked down hair and remarked rather proudly, "I reckon it might have something to do with my weight. I tip the scales at an even two-sixty — stripped."

"Good lord, Porky, it's a wonder you don't tip the scales clear over."

"Don't make any mistakes," Sullivan said earnestly. "It ain't all fat. I still got some muscle left from my fightin' days."

"What was wrong, couldn't you take it?"

"For quite a spell I took it, but I reached the point where my jaw couldn't. So I got sensible and come out here, opened this place."

"So now we're acquainted, maybe you'll explain why that customer who was in here took off like the devil was after him."

"Don't you really remember, Dix — er — I'm sorry, Santone — guess maybe you couldn't expect to know anything about Faxon. But you — I mean, Dix Ryder, run him out of town once, something over five years back. Told him Dix'd let daylight through him, if Dix ever laid eyes on him again."

20

"Oh. This Dix Ryder must have been quite a gunfighter —"

"But always on the side of the law," Porky insisted emphatically. "Arboledo was once a mighty hard town. Dix Ryder cleaned it up. There wa'n't no regular law here those days — just a weak-spined marshal —"

"I wonder that that Faxon hombre had the nerve to come back —"

"Oh, a lot of the old wild gang returned, after we heard Dix Ryder was dead. Things are getting a mite rough around here again."

"If some of the old wild bunch is back, maybe that explains why I was getting some particularly sharp looks as I rode through town. There were four hard-looking hombres on your porch when I entered. Two of 'em took off fast, the instant they saw me. The other two tossed me some ugly looks."

Porky nodded. "Yeah, I know who you mean. They were in here a while back. I remember now that two of 'em were run out by you — er, Dix — about the same time as Faxon. They're some of the same scuts that come back here — later. So you really ain't Dixon Ryder, eh?" There was a pleading note in Porky's voice.

21

Austin shook his head. "Never even heard of him over Texas way. I met a feller once in Fort Worth who looked something like me and folks got to thinking we might be cousins, or some other relation. But we weren't, so far as I knew, or him, either. Right nice cuss, too."

"Nor no relation to Dix, even?"

"Not so far as I ever knew. Could be, of course, we'd be distant relations, if you say I look so much like Ryder."

"Look like him?" Porky snorted. "So help me Hanner, you could pass for him, any place. I noted when you first come in — same easy stride. Hair and eyes and chin identical, same sort of manner. When I first laid eyes on you I forgot all about Dix being dead. Of course, you look, mebbe, five years or so older than Dix, but then Dix would look older by this time, too — if he'd lived."

"Some of the wild bunch kill him?"

"That was suspected, but never proved. He just up and disappeared one day. Later came proof he was killed down in Mexico —"

"Proof?"

"So far as everybody else was concerned, but the Doctor never would believe it."

"The Doctor?"

"Dix Ryder's wife — a girl doctor. She wasn't really a doc. She'd been studying in a medical college when her health sort of gave way, and she came out here to recover. The hotel wa'n't no place for a pretty gal to stay, so Dix Ryder's mother took her in. Anyway, when Dix's mother died, Dix married her. She was right good at fixin' up gunshot wounds and so on. We always called her the Doctor, and as the Ryder Ranch ran the DR brand, we got to calling Dix's spread the Doctor Ranch."

"She must have recovered all right?"

"Sure enough. She was all okay before she'd been out here a year. You should see her today."

"I'd like to, but I won't be around here long enough. I'd figured to stay at your hotel overnight, but I reckon now to be drifting along."

"Sure wish you could stay," the fat man said wistfully. "We could have a lot of fun foolin' people. They'd believe you was Dix, fast enough."

Austin shook his head. "That's what I'm afraid of. If some of Ryder's old enemies are back in town, I wouldn't want to find myself stopping a chunk of lead — and some fellers today sure thought they were seeing Dix Ryder — some of 'em friendly, others just the opposite, it appeared like."

"And that would be natural. But by this time they'd have come to their senses and remember that Dix wasn't alive any more. But I'll bet a pretty that for a minute they was as shocked as I was." He paused a moment. "Well, the laugh is on me. I reckon I owe you a drink, or a cigar, or something."

"I'll take a cigar, thanks."

Porky reached to his back-bar and produced a box of Havanas. Austin extracted one of the weeds, smelled it, bit off one end and placed it in his mouth. Porky scratched a match and held the flame with a hand that still shook a trifle from the shock he had had.

"Hope you like that smoke," the barkeep said. "It was a favorite of Dix's." He looked a trifle sheepish. "I've always kept a box on hand — sort of for sentimental reasons, I guess."

Austin exhaled a plume of gray smoke. "Dixon Ryder," he stated, "sure had a prime judgment in good tobacco. I'd like to hear some more about those enemies he cleaned out."

He awaited an answer. Porky didn't reply at first. When he did he changed the subject. "Now will you have a drink on the house?" he offered.

Santone Austin didn't miss the evasion, nor the fact that Porky's eyes weren't quite meeting his own. "Reluctant to talk, Porky?" he asked.

"Reckon mebbe I've already talked too much," Porky stated directly. "I want to stay healthy."

"Meaning it's not healthy to talk against Dix Ryder's enemies."

"Now that they've grown powerful in Arboledo again," Porky admitted frankly. "It might not be smart to shoot off my mouth too much. It might get back to Wick — er — to some other party. For a spell here we had a rather epidemic of lead poisonin'."

"And you couldn't find a medic to diagnose or cure the trouble?"

"You can't cure dead men who've been plugged in the rear by unknown killers. We could some of us guess at who did the killin' — but guessin' ain't proof. Without proof and a fast gun, a feller had best keep his lips padlocked."

"Sounds sensible," Santone Austin conceded. "I was just interested to hear what was going on. You could call it idle curiosity. So don't spill anything to me, if you feel you should keep quiet."

"Mebbe I've already said too much," Porky said uneasily.

"You don't need to fret your head about me," Austin smiled. "I'm not one to shoot off my mouth. Anyway, I'm just riding through."

"Not even going to stay the night in Arboledo?"

"I've changed my mind about that. Like I said, I don't want to be mistaken for this Ryder man and take a lead slug in the back."

"You on some sort of cattle-buying trip, or looking for a job?"

Santone Austin shook his head. "Neither."

Porky shrugged bulky shoulders. "Could be you don't want to talk too much, too. That I can understand. I reckon that was just some idle curiosity on my part."

"That's all right with me. But I'm through buying cattle for a time, and I'm not looking for a job. Nope. I'm just riding. Sold my outfit over in Texas and decided to take a vacation. Never been in Arizona Territory before. I'm just riding — riding and looking for what's to be seen beyond the next range. It's a disease I got, called itching hoof. There's nice country hereabouts."

"You're right. Fine grazing and nice folks — mostly."

"You bet. I've been around a lot. To tell the truth some of this Arizona country reminds me of other places I've seen in the past. Guess I'd better be shoving along and see where the next trail leads."

Porky seemed reluctant to see Austin leave. He offered another beer which was refused. Then a cigar, which met with a second refusal.

Finally the hefty barkeep put voice to what he had in mind: "Would it be too much to ask you to do me a favor?"

Austin studied the man. "I might. What have you got in mind?"

Porky said slowly, "So long as you don't intend to stay here, would you mind not telling anybody you're Santone Austin. Just let 'em think, should you stop to talk to anybody, that you're Dix Ryder."

Austin stared at the man. "And catch a slug from behind?" He laughed shortly and shook his head. "Do you take me for a jackass-brained idiot?"

Porky said earnestly, "So long as you're not staying here, I don't figure you'd run any risks. You'll be out of town five or ten minutes after you leave here."

Austin said, "Supposing I was to meet

some of Ryder's old friends? What then?"

"I doubt you will. If you did, pass it off as a joke. I'll explain to any old friends, in a couple of days, just what we agreed on, Mister Austin. Would you do it for me, please?"

Santone Austin looked steadily at the man. "Look here, Porky, just exactly what have you got in mind? I'd enjoy to have you do a mite of explaining *to me, now.*"

"Well, you see, Dix's enemies never have been quite sure that Dix is dead. If they thought he was back it might throw a scare into them and quiet 'em down a mite for a spell. And there's a certain scut named Wickmann who needs checking, before he and his scum take the whole town over."

"Hmmm." Austin considered the idea. "You don't know who killed Ryder?"

Porky shook his head. "He just disappeared one day. Then later we got word — and some proof — that he was killed down in Mexico. That is, there was proof of his death, though Dix's wife would never believe he was dead. There was rumors somebody had beat him to the draw. If so, the feller must have been fast with a hawg-laig, because Dix had speed to burn, hisself. The question is, Mister Austin, will you do it?"

"You mean, let on that I'm Dix Ryder, should I meet any of Dix Ryder's enemies?"

"That's the ticket," Porky said enthusiastically. "Just act sort of tough-like should anybody look like he's on the prod for you, before you get out of Arboledo. With Dix's old rep to back you up, I don't figure you'll have any trouble. Gosh, it would be great if we could run a bluff like that on Wickmann and his crew of buzzards."

A slow grin formed on Austin's bronzed features, as he reached a sudden decision. "All right, Porky, I'll do it," he replied. "If you think it will help, I'm willing to do that much for you. Just make sure you don't let the cat out of the bag before I'm well away from this section, or your scheme will fall apart."

Austin turned away from the bar and headed for the swinging doors of the entrance. Just as he reached the doorway, Porky called after him in a loud voice:

"Come in again soon, Dix. I'm sure glad to see you back in town."

Austin glanced over his shoulder. Porky winked widely, motioning with one thumb toward the saloon porch. Now Austin remembered the two rough-looking characters and the two Mexicans who had been

29

on the porch when he entered the saloon. He was suddenly conscious of the glares of hate that had greeted his arrival, and the manner in which one of the men had snapped at the Mexicans' words of welcome.

Austin nodded to Porky that he understood and replied in a clear voice, "I'll get in again as soon as I can, Porky. I was glad to be back, too, as you'll realize."

He pushed through the bat-wing doors and stepped out to the porch. The two Mexicans were gone now, but the other two remained, as though awaiting his exit. Both were giving him hard looks as though inviting some sort of action.

Austin looked steadily at them a moment and smiled thinly. "You two," he stated coldly, "look as though you were waiting for some sort of accident to happen. Anything in particular on your minds?"

One of the men dropped back to the chair he'd just vacated. The other remained standing, one hand nervously stroking an unshaven chin. "Don't get us wrong, Dix," he said hoarsely. "We was just a sort of welcomin' committee to tell you we're glad to see you back."

Austin laughed. "Do you expect me to believe that?" he jeered.

"Aw, don't get us wrong, Ryder," the seated man protested. "We —"

"I doubt I could get you any other way," Austin said scornfully.

"Aw, that's no attitude to take," the seated man said in hurt tones. "Now that Arboledo is plumb peaceful, can't we let bygones be bygones, and forget our old troubles so long ago?"

"So long as you act decent, I probably could," Austin replied. "I didn't come back to start trouble so it's up to the trouble-makers around here to behave themselves — and that goes for your boss, too. You can give him that message from me. Just don't rile me any more and we'll get along hunky-dory, hombres."

The faces of the two men reddened, but neither of them said anything. Austin looked the two over slowly, extreme dislike in his gaze, until their eyes dropped. Then he laughed contemptuously and strode across the plank sidewalk to his waiting horse, and tightened the saddle cinch.

There weren't many people on the street at this hour when the heat of the afternoon sun kept most people indoors, though one man in passing had noticed the three on the saloon porch and realizing something was wrong, kept glancing back over his shoulder as he strode along.

Austin heard one of the men say, "Come on, let's go inside and get a drink." The words were spoken, more loudly than necessary which was a warning to Austin, and he glanced up suddenly to see the bearded individual just dropping one hand to gun butt.

Austin's right hand flashed to holster. His forty-four flashed out and up, covering both men standing on the porch, even before the bearded one could jerk his weapon from holster.

The jaws of both men dropped in dismay. The bearded man's hand left his gun butt suddenly, as though he'd touched something red-hot. Looks of fright crossed the faces of both, and they stared dumbfounded at Austin.

"Just making sure your gun was in holster, I suppose," Austin laughed coldly. "Or did you have some other idea in mind?"

"What — what the hell," the bearded one stammered. It was a very red beard. "We wa'n't startin' nothin' —"

"You reached for your iron," Austin snapped.

"Cripes, that was just force of habit, I expect. Didn't mean nothin', really —"

"Then it's a damn bad habit to have," Austin told him sternly, "unless you can pick up a mite of speed. I've never seen such a clumsy draw and slow! You've had over five years to get some speed. Or maybe you don't need speed to shoot folks when their back's to you."

"Aw-aw —" sputtered Red-Beard. "You — you just thought —"

"Shut-up!" Austin barked. "I heard you say you wanted a drink. Go on inside and get it — but you'd better make it sarsaparilla. All that whisky you've been stowing away not only gives you a purple nose, but it's slowed down your draw something terrible. Go on now, scat, both of you!"

Like a pair of frightened curs, the two men turned and slunk through the saloon doorway, Austin's contemptuous laughter following them.

The altercation hadn't gone completely unnoticed. There had been sudden yells along the street and a few men came on the run. Then, Austin heard somebody yell, "It's Dix Ryder!" Others took up the cry:

"Ryder's returned!"

"Dix Ryder is back!" Yelling resounded along the street.

Someone started a cheer that went

echoing along the thoroughfare. Booming tones split the air: "Hey, Dix, pull up a minute!"

"Where in Gawd's name you been, fellow?"

More cheering. Men were closing in from all directions, booted feet thudding along plank sidewalks, and cries of "Dix! Dix! Dix," came tumbling from enthusiastic throats.

But Santone Austin, face reddening, was already in the saddle and spinning the roan gelding fast.

"Cripes A'mighty!" he told himself. "I got to get away from here — right now! No telling what this might lead to. This just isn't my day for being sociable."

Cramming the Colt's forty-four back into his holster he jabbed spurs into the horse's ribs, the animal hoofing up dust and gravel as it tore off down the street, rapidly carrying Austin out of Arboledo, as frantic cries of "Dix! Dix!" followed in their wake.

Chapter III

Beyond the edge of Arboledo with the last houses some distance to his rear, Austin reined the horse to a gentler gait. Lifting the blue bandanna at his throat, he mopped the beads of perspiration from his forehead. The horse moved into a lazy lope. Here, the trail from town swung toward the northwest. Ahead lay a long stretch of grassy plain, and Austin began to see a few Herefords grazing a short distance off. The plain lifted gradually to the distant purple peaks of the Sangriento Mountains, the summits rugged against the blue sky. Here the trail was plain to follow, marked only with wagon ruts and hoof-chopped earth.

After a time Austin chuckled. "No, I can't blame Porky Sullivan — not for my own stupid actions. But at the time, it semed like it wouldn't do any harm. Trouble is, I never know what to say when folks begin to ask personal questions as what is my business here, and so on, and when a right hombre asks a favor I hate to turn him down."

He mused quietly on this thought a moment before his cogitations continued, "Judging from the reception I got — from both sides — that Dix Ryder must have been considerable of a man. 'Course, judging from the prodiness of those hombres on the saloon porch, I figure I got out of that business right lucky. By cripes! I hope the boys back home never do get wind of that business. They'd hooraw me to a finish."

Abruptly, a fresh idea struck him. "Hell's bells on a tomcat! If I'm not a noodle-headed idiot I don't know! Look what I've went and done. Dammit to hell! Here I've been impersonating a dead man that has returned from the grave. So far, okay, if it could stop there. But what are his folks going to think, if he's got any? Oh, yes, Porky said he had a widow — Doctor Somebody they called her. I don't know whether there's anybody else. Kids, mebbe? Leastwise his widow won't be taking it kindly if she hears I've been passing myself off as her long dead husband returned from the cold grave as the papers say. Said folks, if any, and the widow will just put me down as some sort of skunk. Could be if the news reaches the widow I'll be reviving some sort of hope in her mind

— and then she'll have another let down when she learns the truth. It won't be any joke to her. Good God! What if she's got married again." Austin groaned. "I don't remember if Porky said. Oh, Jeez! When it comes the time to make it tough for other people, I reckon I win first prize. Or, maybe, the booby prize. All I got to do is open my mouth and I put my foot in it. People won't take it kindly if I go 'round making jokes about their dead relations."

He loped on in a bitter, moody silence, severely castigating himself for such fool thoughtlessness, and pondering some means of straightening out the fool mess.

Here and there he passed small clumps of opuntia and sage, now and then an ocotillo. Mostly though, this was fine grazing country with nourishing grass for cattle. Now and then he passed a clump of mesquite. A small stream bordered on either side with cottonwood trees was crossed; Austin lifted his booted feet high while the pony paused to drink. The trail resumed on the other side of the stream. Ahead, Austin could see more timber. Chaparral, perhaps, though it seemed rather high for that species of oak.

By the time the roan gelding had splashed across the stream to the farther bank, Santone Austin had reached a reluctant decision: "There isn't but one thing for me to square myself," he muttered. "I've got to stop off at this dead Ryder's DR outfit and explain matters like a white man should. Like's not his widow will skin the life from me, but maybe I can make her understand how it was. I just hope she — and her outfit, if there's a family — will be the understanding type, and realize I didn't mean any disrespect when I told Porky I'd impersonate Dix Ryder. Anyway, no matter how they take it, I'll feel like I've done my part to clear up any misunderstanding. If they want to get sore, I reckon it just can't be helped."

He swung abruptly into a new trail, heading farther northwest. The trail ahead followed the stream now. There came a slight rise of ground where the stream flowed between steep banks. Austin urged the pony to a slightly faster gait.

"It's a damn' good thing I'm aiming to show this country a clean pair of heels in a hurry, or I might have a scrap on my hands. Still, clearing out this way, a lot of people might get the idea that Dix Ryder was showing a streak of yellow. And I don't like that, neither. Damn it! I wish I'd never stopped in Arboledo!"

By this time he had topped the rise of land. He reined the horse in momentarily to survey the stretch of country spread before his gaze. A long slope descended gradually to rise slightly again, about two miles farther on. The trail was getting into the foothills of the Sangrientos. Abruptly, Santone Austin's lips parted to allow an involuntary exclamation of admiration at the sight which met his eyes.

Half way up the opposing slope was a ranch house with long fronting gallery, built in the form of a hollow square. From the rise of ground where he sat his horse, Austin could see down into the patio, enclosed by surrounding walls, where a huge cottonwood tree spread leafy branches, furnishing welcome shade during hot weather.

The house itself appeared to be constructed of adobe, white-washed, with slightly-sloping red tile of Mexican manufacture, forming the roof. "Gosh!" Austin muttered, "it must have cost a heap of cash to freight that tile and adobe in, or could be Ryder hired some Mexes to make it right on the spot."

He was still a short distance from the house when he slowed down and slipped from the saddle, taking the gelding's rein in one hand. "I reckon," he mused, "it might be best if I just led my horse in, rather than come riding in like I had a right to be here."

He was only a few yards from the house with no one yet in sight. Then a slight noise caught his attention. The front door leading to the wide gallery had opened. A girl had appeared in the open doorway, and took a tentative step onto the gallery. Then she stopped abruptly, raising one hand to her mouth as though to stifle a scream, gazing unbelievingly at Austin. Then she took another step and another . . .

And then she was running toward him, her skirt whipping frantically about her slim ankles. "Dix! Oh, Dix!" she cried, a sob breaking through the tones. "You have come back! I knew you would!"

Austin raised one hand to prevent what she was about to say, so that he could explain matters, but somehow the words wouldn't come. He gulped hard but could only stand and stare at the girl coming toward him. Something about her seemed to stifle speech. She was nearly as tall as he, with cornflower-blue eyes and neatly gathered hair the hue of burnished mahogany, features pulsating with the glow of health, lips red and welcoming. She was dressed in a pale green gown, the bodice accenting the smooth, rounding curve of her breasts.

For a moment the girl paused in her advance. "Dix! Dix, aren't you going to . . . ?" The question went unfinished as she came on again, eyeing him as though she were hypnotized.

He was likewise staring, trying to find his tongue, endeavoring to form the proper words, but all that came was a mumbled, "If this isn't all a dream, I'm plain *loco*, lady —"

And then she was close, her arms lifting, the blue eyes misting with tears of happiness. Involuntarily, Austin's arms lifted, gathered her in, holding her close. He felt her lips warm on his own. Somehow, dazed by the girl's actions, he hadn't been able to prevent what happened. Her lips were fierce in their intensity and for a few seconds he felt powerless to resist. The girl's cheek was close to his and she was murmuring endearments.

When her lips sought his again, realization swept through him, and, reluctantly, he caught her arms and forced her back. "Look — look here, lady," he gulped, before she could voice her surprise, "I'm not your Dix. I'm not Dix Ryder." He was still holding the girl at arms' length. Shamed apologies rose to his lips. He mumbled awkwardly, "I — I shouldn't have let you do that. You see, I — well, it's all my fault. I guess I must be some sort of lowdown — well, some sort of —" he broke off, stammering. "Well, you see, it all came sort of — of sudden. I was too surprised to — well, maybe you see how it is, lady. I never meant things to happen like this — but, well, I was surprised and you sort of took me off my feet and — and —"

"Dix! What are you trying to tell me?"

"I'm just trying to make you understand. I'm almighty sorry, but I'm not your Dix Ryder. My name's Austin — Santone Austin. This is all a bad mistake. I'm — I'm just sorry it happened. I just aimed to drop off a minute and explain —"

"You're not Dix?" The girl stared unbelievingly at him, blue eyes searching his features intently, unbelief in her face. Her eyes became misty and the red lips quivered. Slowly shaking her head, she murmured brokenly, "You're not my Dix — not Dix Ryder?"

"No, ma'am, I'm Santone Austin. Some folks in Arboledo made the same mistake, and I just came out here to sort of explain how sorry I am."

Austin felt his words were idiotic. Something else was needed, but at the moment he couldn't find the proper words, the phrase that would dispel the misery in the girl's blue eyes. He gulped uncertainly, standing with bared head before her, feeling like a criminal on trial.

The girl just stared at him. All the blood was drained from her features now. The misty blue eyes strayed from head to foot, taking in every inch of his lean frame. She didn't even appear to hear what Austin was saying, as he stammered out the story of what had taken place in Arboledo.

"You see," he concluded, striving earnestly to make her understand in his lame tones. "I figured to drop by and apologize for impersonating Dix Ryder, just in case it didn't set right with you. And anybody else that might be concerned. But I feel certain I didn't do anything to hurt Mr. Ryder's character. Porky Sullivan had explained some things to me, and I was just trying to help, really I was. But I didn't mean to cause any harm —"

He broke off, feeling that his excuses were feeble, futile, where the girl was concerned. She was still staring mutely at him,

43

scarcely hearing what he had said. The blood was drained from her face. Slowly, as though recognizing the hopelessness of her dreams, her eyes closed, and she swayed back.

Austin moved just in time to catch her before she dropped. Again, he held the warm form in his arms, but now it was all different. She straightened up, finally, and moved away from him, brushing tears from her cheeks. "I'm all right now," she told him in lifeless tones. "Thank you. It is I who should apologize. You — you see — for a minute I thought you were my husband — returned to life. It was my mistake. I hope I haven't caused you any worry —"

Her voice faltered as she turned away and slowly moved back toward the house. She didn't speak again. Sombrero in hand, Austin watched her weary progress toward the gallery. Not once did she turn back, but progressed across the gallery and disappeared through the open doorway. Austin gazed after her a moment more. Somehow, the sun seemed to have vanished with the girl.

Replacing the sombrero on his head, he swung back toward his saddle, heaving a long sigh. "I guess that's all," he muttered, and his tones weren't quite steady. "God, what a shock that must have been to her. Me, I went sort of haywire myself there, for a minute when I let her kiss me. I should have stopped that before — no" — defiantly — "I'm glad it happened. It's something I'll remember, long's I live, longer than she'd ever remember it. Well, I've said my say. It's my move."

He climbed into the saddle and wheeled the horse. "Lord! What a woman. A man's woman, so help me!"

Chapter IV

The horse was departing at a swift lope when Austin heard the call that came from the house gallery. The girl was back there again, one hand raised in protest at his leaving.

"Mr. Austin — Santone Austin!" she called. "Come back."

A pleasant thrill coursed through Austin at the girl's throaty tones. He wheeled the horse on a dime, as the saying goes, and gave back five cents change, then loped back to the house. A moment later he was standing at the edge of the gallery, gazing up at the girl.

Her voice was steadier now and she smiled a bit wistfully. "I didn't intend that you should leave. I'd like you to stay to supper. I want to hear your story again — of what happened in Arboledo. I didn't get it all, the first time. I wasn't quite myself for a few minutes."

The blue eyes were pleading with him to understand. One slim, tanned hand came out to him. "I want to know you better,

Santone Austin. You're so much like some-one who was dear to me. You will come in, won't you?"

He tried to tell her he should be on his way, but the words weren't convincing. Neither of them was deceived in the excuses he tried to make. There was some further talk and then Austin found himself standing on the long gallery at her side. His horse, reins dropped over head, stood waiting nearby. Austin found it difficult to find his tongue; he followed the girl's every move. She was nearly as tall as he, slim and erect, maybe five years younger.

He stood dumbly while she moved the chairs about in order to accommodate them on the gallery. Suddenly, coming to life, he leaped forward to help her. Leaving matters to him, she disappeared within the house and within a few minutes returned with two glasses on a tray.

She smiled again as they settled into chairs. "They're supposed to be mint juleps," she was telling him, "but I never could mix them as well as Dix. There's the mint he always insisted on having and he maintained the leaves should never be bruised. I took the contrary view. I think it was our only argument, but I'd learned my way back in the east —" she broke off suddenly. "This is all fool talk, isn't it?" She forced a smile. "Anyway, I'll leave the decision to you."

They sipped the drinks. A smile of satisfaction spread over his tanned features. "Without knowing Mr. Ryder's concoction, I'd say he'd have to work hard to beat this. It's almighty satisfactual."

"Satisfactual?" She looked surprised.

He laughed softly. "I've been told before there's no such word, but it happens to express my feelings about something I like. To put it another way — well, it's mighty soothing to the palate. Is that all right?"

The girl's soft laughter came more naturally now. "It was all right before, Dix — er — Mr. Austin." She rose again, white petticoats swirling about slim legs, and entered the house, returning within the minute with a partly-depleted box of cigars which she offered Austin. He noticed they were the same brand that Porky Sullivan had carried in Arboledo. "These smokes may be dried out by this time," she explained. "But they're all I have to offer. At present."

The cigars were somewhat dry as Austin learned when he lighted one, but he had never experienced such a sense of comfort as when he settled back in his chair, blue smoke mingling with gray to swirl about his head. Right then, he never wanted to move an inch, for the remainder of his days, from the present situation. A long silence prevailed, while he considered the turn events had taken.

"And you were saying?" the girl broke in on his meditations.

Austin flushed. "I'm afraid I wasn't saying anything," he confessed, somewhat flustered. "You see, Mrs. Ryder, I guess I'm just sort of dumb," he apologized. "The truth is, I was just thinking how comfortable you've made me feel — when I didn't know what to expect, after I came here. Everything just happened so fast, my tongue, my thoughts, have been roped down like a thrown steer —"

"I understand exactly. It's been a bit of a surprise all around. Now, please tell me again what happened in Arboledo. I think I'm able to listen intelligently now. I didn't get it all, before."

Austin settled back in his chair and related what had taken place, in and out, of Porky Sullivan's Arboledo saloon. He felt the girl's eyes following his every movement, gesture, and figure of speech. ". . . so you see," he concluded, flushing somewhat, "I wasn't intending to shock you. At the time Porky put the proposition to me it seemed like an all-right idea. He seemed to think it would help. And then, later, I got to thinking how you — and maybe others —"

She cut in swiftly, "There aren't any others — not real close, that is. Friends, of course."

That, too, was a relief to hear, Austin told himself. He went on, "Anyway, I got to thinking how you might take the news that some hombre had been impersonating your husband, and I figured the best thing was to ride out and explain personally what had happened. I certainly never intended any disrespect."

She assented quickly, "Of course, you didn't, Mr. Austin. It's all right. I understand thoroughly. I'm so glad you did it. It might cause — well, certain people to think twice, for a day or so — disrupt some plans —"

"Certain people? Plans?" he puzzled.

"It doesn't matter. Forget what I said. You know, you're so much like Dix, my husband, I don't wonder Porky Sullivan and others made the same mistake I did. Every move, each gesture you make reminds me of Dix."

"If you don't mind," he said awkwardly, "I reckon I'm glad "

The girl didn't reply to that. After a moment she said, again, "It's all, all right, Santone Austin. Don't fret about it a minute."

From time to time he had heard movements of horses, men's voices, some distance back of the house. Then there came the sound of a dish pan being vigorously beaten, then the ranch cook's strident tones: "Come and get it-it-t, before I throw it away-y-y."

"Good grief," the girl exclaimed. "There's cookie's supper call. I'd no idea it was so late. You must be hungry."

The sun had dropped behind the Sangriento Mountains by this time. The formerly black shadows were no longer visible, though daylight still hovered. A cool evening breeze lifted across the range bringing the scent of sagebrush to Austin's nostrils. The girl commented again to the effect she was getting hungry herself and he must be too.

Austin noticed the girl watching him keenly, as though she had something on her mind she'd like to put into words. He shook his head. No, he wasn't hungry. At the moment he was willing to go without eating forever, if he could continue to sit at her side.

He rose to his feet. "No, I hadn't thought about eating, but I'll slope down to the mess table and lift a bait with your crew. Like's not they'll be interested to hear any news I might have picked up on my ride into Arizona Territory. Perhaps I should explain about this impersonating stunt of mine, make sure there won't be any hard feelings."

The girl was also on her feet now, shaking her head. "I'll do any explaining that is necessary — later. I'd like to have you eat in the house, with me — and two of our boys. Both are old hands of Dix's. Not many of the old crew are left, to tell the truth. But those two will be glad to meet you."

She started past him, but Austin said, "Let me go and find them. What are their names?"

"Jeff Dayton and Pete Gratton. But you wait here. I'll go get them. I'd rather the rest didn't see you just yet."

"*Por que* — why?" Austin asked in puzzled tones. "Figure they might make some trouble?"

The girl laughed. "Not at all. It's just — well —" she looked rather uncertainly at Austin. "Well, suppose I explain later. I have an idea we'll talk over, after supper. Is that okay with you?"

"Anything you say is all right with me," he replied. At that moment he couldn't have refused her anything.

She descended the steps from the gallery and headed around the corner of the house, passing a tall prickly pear cactus, whose fruits were already beginning to ripen, on her way. Austin settled back in his chair. "This," he told himself, "is the sort of house I'd like to have — and the sort of wife," he added after a moment. He scowled. "And here I always considered women didn't have any place in my life. Reckon maybe I never met the right woman back in Texas. Wonder what her first name is? She's sure still in love with Dix Ryder's memory. I could see that each time she mentioned his name. He must have been a right hombre, to hold a woman like her."

The girl seemed to have been gone quite a time. A man in cowman togs rounded the house, went to Austin's horse and took up the reins, after nodding to Austin. Austin had never seen him before.

Austin asked, "Where you heading with the pony, mister?"

"Ain't you Missis Ryder's guest?"

"I reckon I am."

"I got orders to put your bronc in the corral."

"Oh, I see. Thanks."

"*Por nada* — for nothing," the cowhand replied. "I follow orders."

"Well, thanks, anyway."

"Don't mention it." The man rounded the corner of the house, leading the horse behind him.

"All right, I won't," Austin laughed after him.

The man ducked back into sight momentarily. "I'll give him a rub-down too, and a feed of oats. And no thanks necessary for that either."

"Accept my gratitude then."

But the man was beyond hearing again.

No sign of the girl's return yet. Austin crushed the fire from his cigar butt with the heel of his booted foot and tossed the fragment of weed from the gallery. He wondered what she was explaining to her crew. "Anyway," he mused, "I'll get to spend the night in the bunkhouse, seeing that waddle took my horse to the corral, and my bed-roll with it. A night here will be satisfactual. Wish I never had to leave." His mind wandered back to the moment he had held the girl in his arms. "Least-wise, she doesn't seem to hold that kiss against me — or maybe she's just forgot it, under the circumstances. I'm not ever going to forget, though —"

The sound of voices at the corner of the house broke off his not unpleasant meditations, and Mrs. Ryder approached the gallery accompanied by two cowhands. They mounted to the gallery, the men eyeing Austin curiously.

The girl performed the introductions: "Jeff Clayton and Pete Gratton — Mr. Austin. Santone Austin. And if you two are amazed, boys, think of how I must have felt."

Both men were eyeing Austin with slack-jawed incredulity, as Austin shook hands with them. Neither of them were more than twenty-seven or -eight. Pete Gratton was dark, inclined to a slim-hipped boniness. Jeff Clayton was a big man, but light on his feet, blond, with a chest like a beer-keg. He looked powerful. Austin immediately liked both of them.

"Just to lessen the shock somewhat, I've told Pete and Jeff what you've told me," the girl was saying. "For the moment, I've said nothing to anyone else, except — except that I have a guest."

Clayton brushed one hairy paw across his vision as though to dispel an illusion.

"If — if Mrs. Ryder hadn't explained," he gulped, "I'd sure have been calling you 'Dix.' It's what I call plumb uncanny."

"And that's the truth right from the hawss's mouth," Pete Gratton drawled, shaking his head. "The spittin' image of Dix Ryder, or I'm a cow-hoofed coyote. Me, I'm flabbergasted!"

"Just so there's no misunderstanding," Austin laughed, "that's all I ask. I may be a spittin' image, except that I don't chew tobacco. And you don't look like you ever toted cow hoofs, or neither coyote yelps. Now if I could just boast some of the qualities I've heard Dix Ryder possessed, along with his looks, I'll not kick."

That broke the ice. The four stood talking a few minutes, before the girl said, "Gracious! Our dinner will get cold. Cookie said he'd bring it right up."

Supper was served in a pleasant dining room by Lucia, a rather pretty half Mexican, half Indian girl of around twenty, with sparkling dark eyes and thick, shiny blue-black hair.

There were steaks and boiled potatoes in their jackets, canned tomatoes, beans, pie, and coffee. All the time they were eating, Austin was conscious of the curious glances cast in his direction by the other two men who appeared hard-pressed to realize Austin wasn't in reality the dead Dix Ryder. The food was good; the coffee strong.

Finally supper was finished and the dishes cleared away by Lucia who retired to the kitchen.

Mrs. Ryder rose and closed the door between the two rooms, explaining, "I'm not sure just how far I can trust Lucia," she said. "She's been with me only a year or so. She never knew Dix, of course. I think she's okay, but I'm not absolutely certain. She's an excellent housekeeper, I'll say that for her, though actually I don't need one. But Dix always insisted we keep a girl, and so . . ." She finished rather lamely, and Austin wondered what was coming next, and why all the secrecy?

Gratton and Clayton were watching him intently now, and Santone Austin was perplexed at their attitude. Exactly what was all this leading to? There was something mighty strange afoot. To cover his neglecting to comment, he reached for his Durham and papers, with the intention of rolling a cigarette. Before he could start, Mrs. Ryder reached over and took the "makin's" from his hand, deftly spilled tobacco into two brown papers and rolled

57

a pair of cigarettes, thrusting one into his mouth and the second between her own red lips.

If he was surprised at her action, Austin didn't show it. But in a day and age when no so-called "decent" woman smoked, it was unusual to say the least. By this time Clayton and Gratton had also produced papers and sacks of tobacco and rolled their own smokes. Austin held a lighted match for the girl, admiring the way in which gray smoke spiraled from her sensitive nostrils. She lifted a fresh pot of coffee that Lucia had placed on the table before leaving, and poured cups full. Still, Austin waited.

Mrs. Ryder began, "I said something about wanting to talk to you. It's really important. I've talked my idea over with Pete and Jeff and they think it might work. You could do me a big favor — a favor I've no right to ask, I suppose."

She paused a moment to adjust the wick on the oil lamp near her elbow, and seemed at a loss for further words.

Austin tried to be helpful: "Well, if there's anything I can do, any favor, just say the word. I'll be more'n glad to oblige."

"Thank you." The girl smiled. "That's a

relief. You may change your mind in a minute. To be brief, Mr. Austin, would you be willing to continue the impersonation a little longer? Pretend you're really my husband?"

"Huh!" Austin's eyes widened, his jaw went slack. "But — but — look here, what's the idea? I rode here thinking I had to explain a mistake and now you want me to carry on with the stunt. I —"

"I'll not blame you if you don't want to," the girl cut in. Again, she seemed at a loss for words, and appealed to the two cowhands: "Jeff — Pete — maybe you can make it clear."

Jeff Clayton took up the conversation, "It's like this, the DR is in a pretty bad fix, and we need help. If we don't get it, Mrs. Ryder is going to be forced to sell out — to a skunk."

"I wouldn't want to see that happen," Austin conceded, waiting to hear more. "This is too nice a place to be run by a — a skunk."

The girl put in, "We think you could help us, Mr. Austin. If you haven't any other connections — I — I well, I don't suppose I have any right to ask. I can't offer you money. Actually, it takes all I have to keep things running as it is. I just manage to meet my payroll for the crew. Jeff and Pete have been kind enough to continue on at half wages until things get better — if they ever do." Her blue eyes misted and she looked away a moment, then she stubbed out her cigarette butt on a saucer.

Austin stepped into the breach. "Look here, Mrs. Ryder," he stated. "I'm foot-loose. I don't need money. Believe it or not, I've got more money right now than I have any use for. I had a spread down in Texas. A feller wanted it more than I did, so I sold out the Monarch to him. He paid plenty —"

"You owned the Monarch spread in Texas?" Clayton released a short whistle of surprise. "Jeepers! That's a big outfit, an old outfit —"

Again, Austin nodded. "That's right. In a way I hated to let it go. But this feller was a millionaire and better, and he bothered me night and day until I sold to him. I got to thinking I hadn't been foot-loose for a long time. I wanted to travel over this way and see what lay west of the Rio Grande. And so, here I am. Available, you might say."

"What became of your crew?" Pete Gratton wanted to know.

"They stayed on with the new owner, but he wasn't too interested in cattle. He and his associates had an idea they could drill for oil, and they felt right sure of bringing it in. Meanwhile they were going to string along with cows for a spell. I could afford to pay my old crew a chunk of wages in advance, when I left, in case they got laid off, but if that's going to be oil country, I wanted to get away for a while. That answer your questions?"

"I've heard there are some likely oil lands over Texas way," Clayton put in. "I was born there — lived there right along until 'bout eight years back. You live in Texas long, Santone?"

"Long's I can remember," Austin replied.

"This isn't explaining to Mr. Austin just what's needed here," the girl broke in. "Pete, how about you saying how things have been?"

Gratton nodded, brushed back his black hair from his forehead. "Something over five years ago, Arboledo was a right nice quiet town. Then a wild bunch started to take over. Things went from bad to worse — until Dix took a hand and organized a bunch of right hombres to fight back. There was a lot of hot lead thrown, but there wa'n't no crook could stand up to Dix Ryder. He run the scuts out of town, after a showdown with Burchard — Ross Burchard. He was head of the bad 'uns. With Burchard dead, the spine of the crooks was broken. We thought it would all be hunky-dory here from then on. Then — then —" Gratton hestated, "well, Dix died. Since then, the old gang he'd run out has been drifting back. Last coupla years things have been on the decline again. Like Mrs. Ryder and Jeff has been saying, the DR is having trouble. We just think if the crooks think you've returned, things will quiet down again. You sure had 'em buffa-loed —" he smiled sheepishly, "that is, Dix sure had 'em buffaloed before, and they may take warning —"

"Look here, Mr. Austin," the girl put in, "as I say, I've no right to ask this. There'll be no cash I can promise you — not right off, that is. There may even be some danger." The corn-flower blue eyes were appealing. "You'd best think it over before you decide to throw in with us."

"I've already been thinking it over," Austin smiled. Impulsively, he added, "All right, I'll do it. I just hope I'll be able to help."

The girl's hand reached for his and he

found himself liking the warmth of the slim brown fingers. The two men gripped his hand, and he sensed they were both men to back him up in whatever play he made from now on.

"There's just one thing," Austin continued, "by this time, Porky Sullivan may have explained that he was just running a whizzer on the town, and my impersonation would be useless. Though he said he'd not tell the truth for a couple of days."

The girl bit her lip. "That's true," she acknowledged. "I've known Porky for a long time. He's solid. But somebody should ride in, right now, and tell him what we plan, and to keep his mouth shut and play along with our bluff. Jeff — Pete — one of you should —"

Pete Gratton pushed back from the table. "I'll saddle up and stir some dust pronto into Arboledo, and get to Porky before he can do any wrong talking." Seizing his sombrero, he walked with long strides from the dining room, out through the kitchen.

Now, Austin took over. "The first thing I'd best do is slope down to the bunkhouse and meet the rest of your crew. Who's your foreman?"

"Man named Ridge — Hugo Ridge."

"Good man?" Austin asked.

"The longer he stays here, the less I like him," the girl stated bluntly. "After Dix was gone I tried to carry on alone for a while. There were things I couldn't do that a man could. Somebody in town recommended Ridge and I hired him. I was pretty well mixed up, those days, not thinking straight. I should have appointed Jeff, here."

"Me?" Clayton looked surprised. "But I hadn't had any experience running a crew. I can't blame you for grabbin' at the first chance that came along."

"I should have taken a better chance," she said flatly. "How we'll explain your absence, Mr. Austin, I don't know, but —"

"We'll figure that out later." Santone Austin rose from his chair. "C'mon, Jeff, we'll slope down to the bunkhouse and meet the crew. I want to get established as Dix Ryder soon's possible — and you'd best remember to be sure to call me 'Dix,' from now on."

"That's going to be easier than calling you 'Santone,' " Jeff Clayton laughed.

Chapter V

The two men passed through the kitchen and out into the enclosed patio. The sky was dark, fairly powered with stars, when Austin glanced up through the leafy boughs of the spreading cottonwood tree.

"I was right," Austin laughed.

"About what?" from Jeff Clayton.

"Had a hunch there should be a well under this tree." He indicated the rock-constructed hollow cylinder a couple of yards from the furrowed tree-trunk. "And there it is."

"Oh, yeah. We get real good water hereabouts."

They left the patio through a wide, wrought-iron gate at the rear and continued on toward the long low bunkhouse, some yards distant. Yellow light gleamed from the windows and through an open door, throwing rectangles of illumination across the rocky earth, where booted feet and hoofs discouraged the growth of any grass.

The bunkhouse was a long roomy affair

with a double tier of bunks built along the far wall. Three square wooden tables, surrounded by straight-backed chairs occupied the plank floor. Beneath a window in one wall was a built-in desk for the foreman's use. A half-dozen oil lamps were suspended from brackets about the four sides of the room. A few pictures, clipped from magazines, and two packinghouse calendars provided decorations.

Rolled blankets were in a few of the bunks. Some bits of harness, a cigar box holding some odds and ends, and a dingy pack of cards cluttered one table. Five men in cowman togs, sombreros shoved to the rear of heads, sat at another playing seven-up.

Jeff Clayton whispered an aside to Austin, just before they reached the doorway. "None of the crew ever knew Dix Ryder before he died, so I don't reckon there'll be any difficulties. Come on."

The five men at the card table glanced up as Austin and Jeff Clayton entered, scrutinizing the face of the newcomer. One of them scowled, Hugo Ridge, the foreman, a big, loose-lipped, unshaven individual, in worn corduroys and blue flannel shirt. Something about him instantly frayed on Austin's nerves. Ridge sneered,

"So the Lady Boss's pet cowpoke is back among us workin' hands again, Clayton. Where's Gratton?"

"He had to ride into town —"

"Thought I heard a hawss leavin' a spell back —" Ridge broke off. "What'd he go to town for? He never got no permission from me —"

"You'll have to ask Mrs. Ryder 'bout that," Clayton replied quietly.

"I aim to do just that," Ridge growled. "There's been too much disruptin' 'round here, as it is. I don't aim to have no female interfering with my crew, owner or no owner." His scowling glance took in Austin surveying him from head to foot, then to Clayton, "Who's your friend? One more saddle-tramp to bed and feed, I suppose. No wonder this outfit's losin' money."

Clayton ignored that last. "Boys," he said, clear-voiced, "I reckon you never met Mr. Ryder. He's back at last."

The men struggled to their feet, laying down cards — all except Hugo Ridge who sat glaring in some surprise at Austin. Before he could speak, as the men came forward, Clayton named them and they shook hands. "Amber Odell — our horse wrangler." Austin remembered him as the man who had come after his horse.

Austin looked at Odell, smiled. "I'll thank you now for the rub-down anyway."

"Aw-w, that's all right, Mr. Ryder." Odell seemed somewhat abashed.

"Forget the 'mister,'" Austin laughed. "I'm always 'Dix' to my men." He added, "To *my* men."

Clayton went on, "'Lonzo Tidwell." Tidwell was a rather shambling character with small muddy eyes and a once-broken nose that had been poorly reset. Austin shook hands and went on to the next man.

"Dusty Rhodes." Rhodes was young, with a lean muscular jaw, sandy complexioned. He had a firm muscular grip.

Clayton continued, "Flapjack Hannan — our cook."

Hannan was a wizened-looking old root with a gnarled frame, and scraggly mustache of an indiscriminate gray. He thrust out one bony claw.

Austin said, smiling, "So you're the old coot that spoils grub around here since I left."

"Ain't spoiled no grub," Hannan said defiantly. "If I ain't the best cook in this hull territory, I'll eat my blankets."

"Must have been a chunk of blanket I found in one of my biscuits this evening," Austin said seriously.

"Not so — ain't so a-tall," Flapjack stated stubbornly. "You won't find a cleaner cook in a year's search."

Austin laughed. "You're right, of course, cookie. I was just joshing a mite. If you cooked that supper I had tonight, it was right tasty — best I've had in a coon's age."

Thus mollified, the oldster mumbled, "If you say so, Mr. Ryder. Thanks."

"Make it 'Dix.' "

"Right, Mr. — er — Dix."

"And," Jeff Clayton went on, somewhat sarcastically, "the gentleman at the table over there is our foreman, Mister Hugo Ridge."

Austin looked toward Ridge. The man met the glance with a sneer, saying, "Just what sort of whizzer you trying to run on us, feller? Dix Ryder was reported dead five years back. What kind of crooked rope you tossin', anyway? You figurin' to make some time with Mrs. Ryder. Well, you can't fool me —"

That was as far as he got. In swift strides Austin crossed the floor, seized Ridge's shirt-front and lifted him bodily from the chair. Ridge slashed one burly hand across Austin's wrist, trying to break the grip that was holding him erect. Austin's other hand flashed across, slapping Ridge sharply across the face, momentarily taking all the nerve from the man. He slumped back, eyes wide with fear.

"You stand on your feet when you talk to me," Austin said sternly. "And be damned careful what names you fling around so careless. You got that through your stupid head?"

"Ye— yes, sir, Dix —" Ridge faltered.

"Mr. Ryder, to you, Ridge. Don't forget it! From now on, when we meet, I'm Mr. Ryder. You hear?"

"Yes, sir, Mr. Ryder."

Austin's voice quieted. "Just so you understand. Now we can get to business. The report of my death was in error. If you don't believe I'm alive, try to get proddy with me again. Meanwhile, on the way down from the house, Jeff Clayton stated the DR has been losing some stock while I was away."

"Yeah — that's right," Ridge said reluctantly.

"Why?" Austin snapped.

"Why?" Ridge appeared to not understand. "We— well, cows always — well sort of disappear."

"Cow thieves?" Austin pursued.

"Uh-uh-well, no, I wouldn't say it was

70

rustlers. More like Injuns."

"Indians? What Indians?" Austin jerked out.

"Them Cherry-Cow 'Paches —"

"Chiricahua Apaches? What about 'em?"

"They rob the stockmen all the time. They'll come raiding and sneakin' in, during the dark of the moon. Then you lose anywhere from ten to thuty head at a grab. They're gone before you realize it. Why only a coupla months back there was a bunch of Mescalero 'Paches come raiding clear over from New Mexico —"

"They come this far?"

"Can't say for sure," Ridge said sullenly. "I figure it's them dirty Cherry-Cows —"

Somebody snickered. Ridge looked angrily about but failed to identify the man. He jerked back to attention when Austin said, "All right, that's settled that we're losing stock through thieves — whether they're Indians or not, you say you don't know for sure."

"I'm right sure it's 'Paches."

"What makes you so sure?" Austin asked. Ridge scratched his head and finally admitted he had no proof. Austin flashed his next question, "Why haven't you stopped the thieving?"

"It's too much of a job for a small crew like I got."

"Oh, I see. Did you ever appeal to the Cattle Association for help. They could have sent a couple of men —"

"I suggested that once," Jeff Clayton put in. "Ain't that right, Hugo?"

Reluctantly, Ridge admitted that was right. "But I like to clean up my own range, myself, 'thout callin' in outsiders," he stated in defense of his actions.

Austin didn't trust the man. He said next, "I want to see your account book, tally book and so on, Ridge."

"You'll have to wait a couple days, then, Mr. Ryder," Ridge mumbled. "I been too busy to work on 'em for a spell now."

"Why?"

"Been busy tryin' to run down rustlers."

"What steps have you taken?"

"I've split the herds up — keep 'em movin' around the range to different spots. Ain't got enough riders to watch all them bunches at once —"

"Good way to gaunt up the beef too," Austin pointed out. "Move cows too much and they lose weight. Come beef-round-up they don't bring so much cash. Don't you know that?"

"It's the best thing I could think of.

Why, I even saddled up more'n once and rode herd myownself."

"Hope you didn't get all tired out," Austin said caustically. He turned to Alonzo Tidwell. "Tidwell, do you think the rustling can be stopped?"

"Not a chance," Tidwell said promptly. "Them sneaky Cherry-Cows is too smart. With the few hands we got, a man can't be everywhere at once. Them Injuns spy out the land and —"

"All right. That's enough." Austin took out a small notebook and stub of pencil and started writing on one of the leaves.

"What you doin'?" Ridge asked suspiciously.

"Jotting down the names of a foreman who can't stop the rustling and the hand who agrees with him. To get acquainted with my crew, y'know, I've got to have something to help me remember those names." Then, "Next man," Austin said pleasantly, turning toward Dusty Rhodes. "How about you? The rustlers got you buffaloed too."

"Ain't no man got me buffaloed," Rhodes said defiantly.

"Glad to hear it," Austin grinned. "You think the cow thieves can be stopped?"

"Never heard tell of any what couldn't

be, if it was went at right."

Austin chuckled. "Ever do any cow thieving yourself?"

Rhodes flushed. "No, I never."

"But considered it, eh?"

Rhodes hesitated, then nodded. "The way things look around here, it looks soft," he half-grinned.

Austin liked the young puncher's frankness. "You ride a straight trail, son, and it will look even softer. If you think the thieving can be stopped, how come — in your opinion — the DR has been losing stock?"

"Ask Hugo Ridge," Dusty Rhodes said promptly. "I've never been near any point where stock is stolen —"

"What the hell — !" Ridge commenced angrily.

"Dusty and I are doing the talking, Ridge," Austin clipped the man short. "I already heard your side." He turned back to Rhodes. "You hinting that Ridge knows something about the business?"

"I didn't say that," Rhodes replied. "What I mean was that Ridge always kept me ridin' the draws in the Sangriento Mountains looking for strays. Damn few I found too. I was never put on any night herdin' —"

74

"That's all you're good for, ridin' for strays," Ridge snarled. "A younker like you don't know nothin' about real cow work. You ain't never yet earned your wages —"

"You're a liar," Rhodes snapped, as Ridge started toward him.

Austin shoved Ridge back. "Take it easy, now. This is no time for a ruckus." Ridge subsided. Rhodes glared at him. Austin continued quietly, "Ridge, you say that Rhodes doesn't make a hand. Who hired him?"

"Why — why I did," Ridge admitted.

"So much for your judgment of men," Austin said pleasantly. He scanned the page in his small notebook. "I guess that settles it, Ridge. You're out."

"What do you mean I'm out?" Ridge demanded.

"Out. Done for. Fired. Discharged. Canned. Sacked. In plain words you are no longer on my payroll. I don't want you on my payroll. The same goes for you, too, Tidwell. You go fork your hobby-horse some place else."

Tidwell looked blank, stunned. Ridge blustered, "Well, this is one hell of a note —"

"I understand how you feel," Austin smiled. "You don't like it. Well, I don't like what's gone on in my absence, either. So, get out, both of you — scoot, *vamanos*, make tracks, on your way. And the sooner, the better. I'd appreciate some clean-smelling atmosphere around here —"

"By God, I don't leave until my wages is paid for this month," Ridge yelled. "That goes for Tidwell, too. I stand on my constitootunal rights."

"You mean, constitutional? Hell's bells! Ridge, you're lucky to be standing at all. Your under-pinning looks weaker to me every minute, when you use that tone of voice in speaking to me. How much you and Tidwell drawing a month? And don't lie to me."

Ridge's voice became humble. He mentioned the two sums due. Austin glanced at Clayton. Clayton nodded the sums were correct. Austin delved into one overall pocket and came up with a large roll, peeled off a few bills and handed them over, adding, "Anything due anybody else will be paid tomorrow. Odell, how about you — satisfied that stealing can be stopped, and with your job?" Odell mentioned that he'd like to be riding the range more, and not be kept at the corrals, looking after horses all the time. "That'll be taken care of, Amber," Austin told him.

76

He shot a sharp glance at Ridge and Tidwell. Taking the hint, the two hurried their movements.

As they were leaving, Ridge bellowed angrily, "You ain't heard the last of this, Ryder — er — Mr. Ryder."

"Fine," Austin grinned. "I'll do a better job on you next time." He looked at Clayton. "Jeff, we'd best be getting back to the house."

He and Clayton were crossing the patio when Clayton said, "Now, there'll be the trouble of finding a new rod, I suppose."

Austin shook his head. "No trouble. I already hired a foreman."

"You have? Who — ?"

"You. Providing that's all right with Mrs. Ryder. She said she should have appointed you long ago."

"Well, judas priest! I don't know how to thank you, Santone — er — uh — Dix —"

"Dix, it is, Jeff. It'll be a good name to carry — for a time."

Chapter VI

Lucia was nowhere to be seen as the two men entered the house through the kitchen. They heard Mrs. Ryder's voice hailing them from the front of the house, and found her in the big room that stretched clear across the front wall of the building. Here, there was an oil lamp with a soft shade on a table, and a fire of mesquite roots burned cheerfully in a wide fireplace of native rock. Animal-skin rugs were stretched on the floor and the furniture was deep and comfortable. On a low table a bottle and glasses awaited them, near the fireplace. Mrs. Ryder poured two drinks and added hot water as they entered.

"A hot toddy to take the chill off," she smiled, as they seated themselves. Austin made a comment and the girl said, "No, thanks, I don't care for any. Well, Dix — it's still Dix, isn't it?" And when he said it was, she continued, "Did you meet your crew?"

He nodded. "I already fired two of 'em —"

"Jeepers, Mrs. Ryder," Jeff Clayton burst in. "Santone — that is, Dix, really took hold in a hurry, like he was really head-man. There was no trouble pullin' the wool over the eyes of that gang. They're convinced Dix has returned."

"But whom did you fire?" the girl asked.

"Your foreman, Ridge," Austin replied. "I didn't like the looks of that hombre, atall. I figured it best he be on his way. Him and Tidwell. A pair of scuts I figure 'em both, and the DR will be the gainer with them gone. I can't prove it, but I think Ridge knows where your cows are disappearing to. His account books aren't up to date, and he seemed to maneuver cows where they can be picked up easy, if not run to death, shifting them around —"

"I owed them both money," the girl stared. "I —"

"I took care of that," Austin cut in. "We can square accounts later. Your cook I'm sure is all right. So's Dusty Rhodes. I figure that youngster could go a bit wild without a strong hand on his rein, but he's got spirit. I like him. Odell is okay. So there you are. We'll have to see about finding some other hands too —"

The girl said, "I don't like the idea of you paying out your money, when I can't repay you, now. I don't want to add to my obligations, when you've already taken on so much —"

Austin's soft laugh interrupted the words. "Haven't I already told you I have more than I know what to do with now? Paying off those two scuts is just part of the act, Mrs. Ryder. Like I said, we can settle the accounts later, if you'll feel better."

Jeff Clayton put in, "Saying that we'll have to hire more hands is easy — but where we going to get 'em?"

"There's generally cowhands out of work hanging around," Austin stated. "I reckon to pick 'em up."

"Could be you'd have trouble findin' 'em," Clayton replied. "Most of the hands I'm acquainted with have jobs with other outfits hereabouts, and aren't likely to leave. Sure, there's fellers around town, but I don't reckon they're the type we want on the DR. Trouble is, men are afraid of Purdy Wickmann —"

"Who's he?"

"The scut I figure is back of this whole trouble. You run him out once — I mean, Dix did. Those days he was working for Ross Burchard who Dix finished, five years back. Wickmann didn't amount to much those days, just a sort of hanger-on with the Burchard gang. Then something over two years back, Wickmann showed up here again. Some place he got some money — I've heard it rumored he was in on a bank hold-up, down in Sonora, Mexico. How true, I can't say, but I can believe it. Wickmann has changed from the old days and become important around Arboledo, got rid of some of his rough manners, and opened an office in town —"

"What sort of office?" from Austin.

"Claims to be dealing in land, real estate, etc. Got a finger in a lot of pies. Lends money at a high rate of interest, and forecloses fast on properties when the owners can't pay up when the cash is due. He's got a gamblin' joint at the east end of Main Street, but only fools continue to play there —"

"Crooked games?"

"So he's been accused of that."

Austin considered. "Looks like folks hereabouts lack fight. What other outfits are around here?"

Mrs. Ryder answered that. "There are just a few small spreads — the Star-Cross, the Rocking-A, and the Bench-Y are the largest of those. Remember this is new country, Mr. Austin. And then there are a few men who just run a handful of cows while they try to farm, as well. We're the largest spread in these parts."

"Those brands you mentioned — would one of those be responsible for your missing animals?"

Clayton shook his head. "I doubt it. I know all the owners. They look honest to me. They're just afraid that Wickmann will start to work on them, so what hands they got, they keep close to their herds. I doubt you'd get any help — hands — in that direction."

"You see," the girl said, "they just think it natural that an outfit run by a woman would go downhill, and think our troubles are over-rated. So long as Wickmann don't tread on their toes, they intend to shy away from our troubles."

"This Wickmann probably figures," Austin said, "that if he can gobble up the biggest ranch, he can pick up the other pieces later. The fools! If they had the sense that God give 'em to start with, they'd realize their safest move would be to join your fight. What else has gone wrong? Men picking gunfights, I'd suspect."

"Yeah, some of that," Clayton nodded, "but we didn't lose any hands in gunfights. It was the dry-gulchin' that was bad. We lost three good men —"

"Ambushed?" Austin said.

"Two hands and a cook," Clayton related. "The two hands hadn't been with us long, but they were good men. They were found out on the range. Our cook — he'd been with Dix for years — caught it one night late on the way back from Arboledo. All three men had been shot in the back. It was tried to be made to look like Apache deviltry."

"How was that?"

In the case of the two hands, each had an Apache arrow stuck in him. A 'Pache lance was shoved clear through the cook. Now, any fool knows if it had been Injuns, those men would have had their hair lifted. So I wa'n't fooled any, but a lot of folks was. And there was a yelp to have U.S. Cavalry sent here. Well, the cavalry come, but they couldn't find anything 'cept peaceful Injuns, so they left. And that's the way it has been going."

"No local law here — sheriff or deputy?"

"We appealed to the county seat," the girl said. "The sheriff there has sent three deputies. Arboledo being small we don't get too much attention. One by one, those deputies decided they didn't want to stay."

"Scared out?" from Austin.

"Either that or bought out," Clayton said grimly. "I tell you, Wickmann has just about taken charge around here. Trouble is, he claims to be friendly and he fools a lot of people. And we've not been able to get any definite proof against him."

"You have any idea exactly what he's trying to get?"

"The DR Ranch," the girl said flatly. "He's offered to buy me out, but never offers much money. I've stalled him off each time, by saying until Dix has actually been proved dead, I can't get probate through the courts and give proper papers for a sale. But he's certain Dix is no more."

"And you?" Austin asked.

The girl sighed and brushed back a lock of shining brown hair from her forehead. "I can't just believe it," she stated stubbornly. "In the first place, Dix suddenly disappeared after he'd settled the wild bunch. Why should he leave abruptly in such fashion, with no word to me? Then about six months after his disappearance, a captain of *rurales*, down in Chihuahua, sent word that Dix had been shot in a gunfight and had been buried there." Mrs. Ryder's eyes misted and for a moment she couldn't continue.

Jeff Clayton took up the story. "You see,

84

this *rurale* captain sent back Dix's clothing, letters, and other things that led to the identification, together with a photo picture of Mrs. Ryder."

"I even went down to Chihuahua," the girl said, "looking for further proof. By that time the *rurale* captain had gone away — no one knew where — nor could anybody remember where the body had been buried. But until I get actual proof, I'll still believe that Dix lives."

Austin marveled at the steadiness of her tones. His throat tightened at thought of her faithfulness, awaiting a husband who'd never return. To brook an awkward moment Austin said, "Well, maybe things will pick up now. One way or another we'll get the cow thieving stopped and see if we can't get the DR back in the profit side of the ledger."

"It's not just the loss of beef stock," Mrs. Ryder said, "though that's bad enough, of course. You see, if Wickmann could get this property, he stands to make a pile of money —"

"Raising cattle?"

The girl shook her head. "Not solely. But there's a rumor that the T.N. & A.S. Railroad would like to lay rails from Arboledo to the northwest. Anyway, there's a rumor to that effect."

"It's more than a rumor," Clayton put in. "There was a T.N. & A.S. representative came here four or five months back, and asked permission to send a team of surveyors here, working across DR holdings."

"So far as we could figure," Mrs. Ryder took up the explanation, "the DR land offers the most accessible route through the biggest pass in the Sangriento Mountains. I'd be glad to see a line go through here, and I'd not ask much for a right-of-way through the property. It would be the making of Arboledo, bring more settlers into the country. But it's my idea that if Wickmann took over here, he'd really stand to make a lot of cash before he gave the railroad a right-of-way. That's the big stake he's playing for, I think. The cattle stealing and killing are just means he takes to try and discourage my hanging on."

"Things are coming a mite clearer now," Austin nodded. "How are you fixed for money?"

Mrs. Ryder shook her head. "We're not fixed," she stated bluntly. "We planned to get a good gathering come beef round-up, but I still think I'll have to raise a loan. The Arboledo bank, considering conditions here, isn't too anxious to lend, and then only at a high rate of interest. Wickmann would be only too glad to get me in his web, but naturally I don't go for that sort of business."

Austin nodded. "Don't let it worry you. When you need some cash, let me know." He grinned. "I promise my interest charges won't break you, and I haven't any web to trap you in." He cut short the girl's attempt to thank him, saying, "If I'm to pose as Dix Ryder maybe you'd better give me a line on old friends I'll have to meet."

"Besides Porky Sullivan," Clayton asked, "who did you run across in town?"

"That's hard to say," Austin frowned. "A heap of people seemed to know me —"

"Everybody in town knew Dix, and practically everyone called him friend," the girl said.

"— and then there were those two plug-uglies in the saloon porch," Austin remembered. "They looked like they wanted trouble, but lacked the nerve to carry it through."

Clayton scowled. "Mrs. Ryder already told me'n Pete Gratton about that. The husky galoot with the red beard like's not is Doag Barbe, a no-good ex-pug. Can't say I can place the other galoot. Likely a

Wickmann thug too."

"Let me see." The girl pondered. "There's a lot of names you won't be expected to remember, men of slight acquaintance. There's Banker Phelps." She described him. Another description followed covering Jim Starr of the Star-Cross Ranch, Chuck Albert of the Rocking-A, and Burt Yocum of the Bench-Y. Austin listened intently, pigeon-holing each name and description as she gave it.

"There are two general stores here now," Clayton put in, "but both have new owners since you — since Dix left. Oh, yeah, you sure will have to remember Finch Orcutt that used to run the general store when Dix was here. He's town marshal here now —"

"So you do have some law."

"Orcutt does what he can to hold things down in town. Something had to be done and he consented to run for office. Wickmann put his own candidate up — Doag Barbe. He's the scut with the red beard, but Orcutt got the most votes. So long as a ballot was secret, folks weren't afraid to turn out and elect the right man. Orcutt's got nerve and he doesn't like the way things are going. Dix and he were close friends too."

Time passed while Clayton and the girl drilled Austin on names, descriptions, idiosyncrasies of people living in Arboledo or nearby. The livery stable came in for discussion and the types who hung around it. A map of the town was drawn roughly in lead pencil so Austin could learn the streets, situation of certain buildings, etc.

"Whew!" he paused once, forehead perspiration beading out. "This is a real chore. If I can remember all this, I'll be lucky."

"You've *got* to remember," she returned, "one slip and people might get suspicious. Now let's run through this again."

And so it went on for another hour. There was a knock at the front door. Clayton answered it. Pete Gratton came in, doffing his sombrero. The girl poured hot water for fresh toddies.

"Yeah," Gratton nodded as he took a seat. "I got to Porky Sullivan before he'd told anybody about the joke him and Santone played. He'll play along with us, of course. He says to tell you, Santone, to come in as soon's possible and he'll give you details on a lot of people you have to pretend to know."

Austin groaned in mock dismay. "Looks like school is never going to end."

89

The girl said, "Heavens! Do you realize it's nearly two o'clock? Class is dismissed."

The men got to their feet. There was an awkward silence, broken by Austin-Ryder. "I'll go down and pick out my bunk, if that Amber Odell remembers what he did with my bed-roll."

Another awkward silence, then the girl said, bluntly, "Pete can bring your bed-roll up to the house, Dix."

His eyes widened. "But I can't stay here — with you —"

"Where else would a returned husband and owner of the ranch stay? This bluff has to be carried through properly. Do you want folks to think we've had a disagreement? There are three bedrooms here —"

"Lucia —" he commenced.

"Lucia has her own room, on the second floor of the hay barn." Mrs. Ryder explained. "Dix had a nice room partitioned off up there, when our first girl was hired. So you don't have to worry about that. Look here, when I first told Pete and Jeff about you, I told them what I proposed to do. They agreed, though reluctantly, that you'd have to live in the house, if we were to carry through the bluff in the right way."

Austin glanced at the two men. They both nodded in agreement.

"But — but what will people say — think?" Austin stammered.

"What people?" the girl demanded. She laughed a bit self-consciously, flushing slightly. "Dix, can't you see there's no other way for us?"

"We-ell, maybe you're right," he mumbled, still not quite convinced she was right in her plans.

Gratton and Clayton started to leave, saying their goodnights. Santone and the girl heard the back door shut and the retreating steps across the patio.

"There's just one thing I think should be straightened out," he said a trifle awkwardly.

The girl whirled back, stiffening a bit. "And that is?" she asked quietly.

"You said," he reminded her, "that I had to live and *be* Dix Ryder. There's one thing I think I ought to know — now."

The girl's cheeks reddened, her chin came up. She looked at him very directly and then relaxed when she saw the corners of his lips were twitching.

"As Dix Ryder," he explained, "I can't very well continue calling you Mrs. Ryder. I think I ought to know your first name."

Her smile answered his. "It's Sabina," she told him.

"Sabina," he repeated, relishing the sound. "It's a nice name. I won't forget it," telling himself, he'd never forget it. "Good night, Sabina." He picked up his bed-roll.

"Good night, Dix."

Chapter VII

It was nearly ten o'clock that same night before Hugo Ridge and Alonzo Tidwell found Purdy Wickmann in the bar of his Gila Chance Parlors. Parlors? A misnomer. Simply a big bare room where certain men presided over dice tables, the wheel, chuck-a-luck, faro tables and other not-so-honest games of chance where "suckers" donated their cash to what might have been termed a lost chance. There weren't any dance-hall girls to lure customers from Wickmann's games. He was a man of single purpose and didn't believe women helped him to his gains to any extent. Women, he figured, only stood for trouble, and he'd get along without them. Well, he must be right; he was doing all right.

He was a tall, lean man, steely muscled, with a bit of a receding hair line and pale blue eyes, set too closely together, as he stood at his bar, slowly working his way through a bottle of warm beer. A sombrero of pale gray topped his head. He wore a string tie and fancy vest, and corduroys, tucked into flat-heeled boots. A coat, known as a Prince Albert, came to his knees. There was no gun in sight, but it was generally accepted that he carried an under-arm gun in a shoulder holster. A long thin cigar jutted from his thin lips, and his black eyebrows seemed to meet in a straight line above his nose. He had very white teeth, but his smile reminded most people of the exposed fangs of a cougar.

The bar was crowded, as a perspiring bartender could attest. From the adjoining room came the sounds of clicking poker chips, the whirring of a wheel and considerable cursing on the part of gamblers who'd lost. With Wickmann was the husky-bodied, red-bearded Doag Barbe, who currently termed himself Wickmann's right-hand man. He held this position simply because Wickmann had been unable to find a better man to fill the bill.

On the other side of Wickmann, stood a somewhat undersized fellow of about thirty, with rather baleful-looking eyes and a surly manner. A product of some slum was Vince Heffner. A police record back east had driven him west where he made a living with his six-shooter. He wore cowman togs and boots, but, aside from some ability to ride, he was no cowman.

He was, in short, a hired killer, as the notches in his gun butt attested. Small, yes. A sidewinder rattler is also small. And deadly. He was eyeing his small tumbler of whisky with some distaste. Whisky always hurt his stomach, he told himself secretly, but he had to, tried to, act the part of a man. Actually, he preferred sarsaparilla, or another type of pop called cherry phosphate. He was childlike in many other ways as well, as went with his retarded brain. He had learned but one trade: kill for cash, and it made no difference to him who the victim was, so long as he was well-paid. Too, he was like the sidewinder — venomous, and in many cases deadly. A type to steer clear of.

Wickmann felt a hand on his shoulder. Turning, he saw Hugo Ridge, with Alonzo Tidwell standing behind him.

"Oh hello, Hugo — 'Lonzo. What you two doing in town? Hugo, you look upset about something?"

"I got a right to be," Ridge growled. "We went up to your place, and you wa'n't there, so then we come here. I got to talk to you. There's hell t'pay."

"That so?" Wickmann said easily. "Oh yes, meet my friend, Vince Heffner. He heard I could always use good men, so

95

when he came to Arboledo today, I hired him."

Tidwell and Ridge put out their hands, but Heffner gave them only a surly nod and turned back to his whisky, wincing when he took another sip of the amber liquid.

"Let's go up to your place. We got to talk," Ridge proposed.

"Anything you got to say can be said right here," Wickmann stated shortly. "What's eating you?"

"There was a hombre named Dix Ryder come to the DR tonight —" Ridge commenced.

Wickmann's laugh cut him short. "You mean to say he had the nerve to ride out there? That feller is up to something. I heard today some feller using that name was in town. A lot of folks think he really is Ryder, too."

"Didn't you have some trouble with a feller called Ryder, 'bout five years back?" Ridge persisted.

"Yeah, but he's dead. Must be this new galoot is a cousin or brother that looks like him. Probably callin' on the Widow Ryder. Why this hombre even has Porky Sullivan thinking he's Ryder. I talked to Porky. He was took in complete. The feller rode out of town shortly later, like's not laughin' his head off at the fools in Arboledo. Forget it. Hugo — 'Lonzo, what'll you have to drink? Then you'd better get back to the DR and keep an eye on things."

"We can't," Ridge said.

"What do you mean, you can't?" Wickmann frowned.

"We been fired from our jobs," Ridge explained.

"T'hell you say!" Wickmann exclaimed. "Mrs. Ryder gettin' uppity all of a sudden?"

"He sacked us — this hombre claimin' to be Dix Ryder."

Wickmann swore an oath. "How does he expect to get away with that sort of deal? Whyn't you tell him to go to hell?"

"Well, I didn't want to kick up no trouble, 'til I'd talked to you —"

"And you sort of lost your nerve, eh?" Wickmann snapped. "What happened — no, wait. We'll go up to my place and talk this business over, where nobody'll hear us. Come on."

Leaving his beer unfinished, he stalked, forehead creased in a frown, from the Gila Chance Bar, followed by Ridge, Tidwell, Barbe, and Vince Heffner who was glad to leave the rest of his whisky untouched.

The long curving street was dark when they stepped outside, except for a light here and there. Their booted feet clumped hollowly on the plank sidewalks. Only a few ponies stood at hitch-racks. Only a solitary figure was to be seen, approaching them, still some distance off.

"Marshal Orcutt," Doag Barbe grunted in a disagreeable tone. "I'd like to plug that bastard sometime."

"Go ahead. I'm not stopping you," Wickmann said sourly. "Just keep me out of it, if you get caught."

Barbe said eagerly, "Why not now? There's five of us and —"

"Five of us," Wickmann snapped. "True. That's why you're so brave. I've got a hunch Orcutt is faster'n you, Doag."

"But there's five of us," Barbe repeated. "The streets are empty —"

"Cut out the fool talk," Wickmann snarled. "I don't want to be tied into any job you do."

Vince Heffner spoke. "A job for me, Mr. Wickmann?" There was a certain eagerness in his tone.

"Not now, dammit," Wickmann snarled. "Behave, the lot of you." He added, "We got one problem to settle first and I want to talk that over and see what's what."

The marshal approached, striding easily along, a tall, spare man with wide shoulders. A badge gleamed dully on his denim shirt, in the light of the stars.

Wickmann said politely, "Evening, Marshal."

Orcutt replied, "Howdy, men."

"Town seems quiet," Wickmann said, as Orcutt continued on.

"And I aim to keep it that way," Orcutt tossed back, as he passed.

No one spoke as the marshal's footsteps died away. Wickmann and his followers continued on, until they came to a two-story false-fronted building, with a flight of steps leading up on the outside of one wall. Wickmann had his living quarters and office on the upper floor; the lower floor was tenanted by a general store, now dark.

At the top of the stairs, Wickmann unlocked a door and they went inside. An oil lamp was lighted. A worn carpet covered the floor. There was a desk, roll-top, with an armed chair behind it. Several straight-back chairs stood about. In one corner stood a heavy iron safe. Against another wall was a bookcase, holding a small library of law books, most of which pertained to legal statutes and jurisprudence regarding land deals. Wickmann laid no claim to being an attorney, but the books were impressive to those who didn't know the man well. He had purchased them second-hand, someplace, and considered the money well spent.

Wickmann sat down in the desk chair. The others found seats. Wickmann said to Ridge, "All right. Tell me exactly what happened tonight at the DR, Hugo."

Ridge told the story, backed up now and then by words from Tidwell. Wickmann's scowl grew heavier as the talk went on. He said, "Why didn't you call his bluff? Tell him you didn't take that sort of talk from no man."

"Hell's bells!" Ridge exclaimed. "I tried. There I was, sittin' back in my chair, defiant as hell, when he walks over and grabs me by the shirt and yanks me up on my feet. And the hombre tells me I should allus call him 'mister' and —"

"And you lost your nerve and you called him 'mister,' if I'm not plumb mistaken," Wickmann snapped. "And then he threw you out without you putting up any sort of argument —"

"Well, geez! Purdy, he's a tough customer. His eyes sort of looked right through me, and — well, it seemed like everybody was on his side, 'ceptin' 'Lonzo, here, and, besides —"

"Stow it, Hugo," Wickmann cut the man short. "And don't neglect to call him *Mister* Ryder, next time you meet —"

"Next time, I'll tell him a thing or two," Ridge blustered.

"In a pig's eye you will! But he's not Dix Ryder, I can tell you. Might be some relation. He took Porky Sullivan in, and Porky's known him for years. I ain't surprised he fooled you into thinkin' —"

"Well, Clayton and Gratton knew him in the old days," Ridge said defensively. "You claimin' he fooled them too? To say nothing of the woman. You mean to say he's pulled the wool over her eyes as well?"

Wickmann grunted. "Like's not, she's in on the game too. But he don't fool me. I know damn' well the original Ryder is dead. Hell! I was there —" Wickmann paused abruptly, then, "Dammit! The authorities in Mexico buried him. They even had proof of identity —"

Doag Barbe said, "I wasn't here those days. It was Chesty told me about him when he first come to Porky's. What happened to the old crowd you've told me about, Purdy?"

Wickmann shrugged, "Most of 'em is scattered from hell to breakfast — headed below the Border when Ryder got the upper hand. I had the guts to come back, and a few others — but most of 'em is just hangers-on, hopin' I'll hire 'em." He grinned. "Well, let 'em. It makes me look that much stronger. The real Ryder was hell-on-wheels. We was runnin' Arboledo, until Ryder got busy. There was a hell of a lot of lead thrun. It was Ryder gunned down Ross Burchard — our boss them days — and plugged another hombre while doin' it. Burchard was no slouch in a gunfight. He was fast, but Ryder was faster. Anyway, Dix Ryder organized a lot of his pals and — I got to admit it — run us out of Arboledo. Most of us scattered down into Mexico. We left word if he wanted to finish the job to come after us. Some of us didn't scare off so easy, but we didn't linger around long. Reckon I'm the only one that had the guts to come back here. But I'm into a new deal, now days, and I aim to keep it that way."

"Folks got respect for you now days, Purdy," Doag Barbe put in with a smirk.

"They damn well better respect me," Wickmann growled, "one way or t'other. Lot of folks owin' me money around here. They realize I can choke 'em off any time. Yeah, they respect me all right."

He asked further questions regarding the man who called himself Dix Ryder. Ridge supplied information. "That sure sounds like the real Ryder," Wickmann conceded, sighing. "So there's another problem staring me in the face, but this fake Ryder don't fool me none. I got a heap more sense than I had five years back. I'm just waitin' to hear what explanation he'll give for being away all this time. I know damn well his excuse won't hold water, and then his whole bluff will be blowed sky-high. So don't let this feller scare you out. I'll handle him. You'll see. I got too big a stake in the game I'm playing now, to give in to him. We'll lick him proper."

"That's the talk," Barbe exulted. "Just let me lay a bead on him and —"

Wickmann snarled, "Close your trap, Doag! Damn' confident now, ain't you? As I heard it, he faced you down on the porch of Porky Sullivan's saloon — you and another gutless wonder —"

"Well, geez! Purdy, he had me covered. I ain't no fool —"

"I'm not certain of that. But I reckon it didn't take much speed to beat you to a draw. You're about as fast gettin' your gun in action as an old woman hangin' diapers on a clothesline. You might have been good with your fists, once — so you say — but you ain't no gun-slinger. Now, take Vince, here — that reminds me, Vince, it might be a good idea to change your sights and keep a line on this hombre pretendin' to be Ryder. For the moment you can forget Clayton."

"You hire Heffner to down Jeff Clayton?" Ridge asked.

"I don't admit I hired Vince for anything but cow work, when it's necessary," Wickmann said smoothly. "But in case he should happen to tangle with Clayton, and was still on his own feet when the smoke cleared away, I wouldn't burst into tears. I figure Clayton's too smart to be healthy much longer."

"Aw, I can handle both of 'em," Heffner boasted, "if you got the cash to pay for two, Purdy. One job's like another."

"Not where Dix Ryder is concerned," Wickmann said swiftly, "— if this phony is as good as Ryder was once. So you work easy and make sure when you meet him."

"Don't care how good he is," Heffner spat, "he don't bother me none. I know I'm better."

"I hope I can take your word for it," Wickmann grunted. "By the way, Hugo, what did you do with that last bunch of steers the Apaches run off?"

Ridge's loose lips curled back in a smile that revealed tobacco-stained teeth. "That 'Pache idea was a good one, eh, Hugo? We got them cows in a box canyon, not too far from here, while we change brands and ear-markin's. With what was took before, we got a right nice herd made up. Then we'll run 'em over the line. There's a buyer down there who'll take all we drive to him. And, Purdy, you'd better make me out some sort of bill-o'-sale, like always, to show a buyer. I figure —"

"You leave all figurin' to me," Wickmann said. "All right, remind me again before you leave. What brand you changing to?"

Ridge told him. Wickmann nodded and went on, "Now that you're no longer rodding the DR, you can give the other boys a hand — you and 'Lonzo. The work will go faster. And when you're riding around, you might pick up some more 'Pache arrows and any other junk that will make folks suspect the Injuns."

"You figurin' to knock off another DR man?"

"Ain't never give over figuring in that direction," Wickmann stated evilly.

Ridge nodded. "I'll do that." He asked, after a moment, "Purdy, just exactly what makes you so certain the real Dix Ryder is dead?"

"That's easy." Wickmann gave an ugly laugh. "I was right there, when the real Ryder got his comeuppance — fact is, I had a hand in it myownself."

Chapter VIII

Santone Austin awoke easily, stretched in the bed. "Santone," he told himself, "it's mighty satisfactual sleeping between sheets again." When had he last slept between sheets? He couldn't remember. "Something else I've got to remember," he told himself. "I'm not Santone Austin any more." He remembered Sabina Ryder's words: live Dix Ryder, think Dix Ryder, *be* Dix Ryder. "So, from now on, I'm Dix Ryder. I mustn't allow myself to think of me any other way." He chuckled. "I wonder how long it'll be before Mrs. — er — Sabina makes a slip. But I reckon maybe she won't; she's got a level head on those trim shoulders."

He glanced toward the shaded window. It was still early yet, he judged. A faint yellow light showed against the shade. He stretched in bed another ten minutes, thinking. Occasionally, a slight frown crossed his face as he concentrated on some knotty problem that was sure to arise. Gradually, his brow cleared. He ran through the lessons that had been drilled into him the previous night, and felt he was letter perfect. It had all been easier than he'd dreamed. By this time he really felt he actually knew the men he was certain to encounter before the day was finished.

Finally he sprang out of bed and raised the shade. Glancing from the curtained window he gathered that the sun had just lifted above the eastern horizon. "Still early yet, so I'll be in time to catch a bait in the mess-house. Wonder what time Sabina gets up. There's still things to talk over with her —"

There came a knock on his closed door and then Sabina's voice: "Dix, there's a pitcher of hot water on the floor out here."

"I'm up. Thanks, Sabina." There, the name had come easily to his lips.

"Yes, I heard you stirring."

He caught her retreating footsteps. "Loss of a couple of hours sleep doesn't seem to bother her," he mused.

He shaved and then prepared to dress. The heavy money belt he'd removed the night before he placed on the dresser. Then he surveyed the clothing in the closet, choosing clean denims and shirt and underwear; a fresh bandanna. The clothes fit him perfectly as did the high-heeled riding boots. He strapped on spurs and chose a well-worn black sombrero. The shaving with Dix Ryder's razor had been welcome: he'd not removed his whiskers in a week.

Breakfast was on the table when he entered the dining room. Sabina was pouring black coffee and gave him a cheery good-morning. He looked admiringly at her. Fresh as a daisy, he was thinking, gazing at her, in some sort of loose blue skirt and blouse, hair neatly brushed and as neatly arranged.

He placed the heavy money belt on the table. She eyed it curiously and continued to serve the food. There were flapjacks, sorghum syrup, bacon and eggs, warm biscuits. She drew up a chair and sat opposite him, after he'd carried the seat to the table, then he settled into his own chair. They began to eat.

"Good Lord, this tastes good," he commented once, draining his coffee cup, which she instantly refilled. "Don't know when I've had a bait to compare to this."

She laughed. "Don't you ever weary of saying that every morning?"

"Nope — never do," he grinned.

She indicated the money belt. "What do you intend doing with that?"

"Put it in your — that is — our bank. There's about two thousand dollars there — gold and big bills. I'll be glad to be shed of all that weight, and then we'll have something to go on, once the *dinero* — money — is in the bank."

She started a protest, but he held up one hand to stop it. She nodded assent and said instead, "I'll get the bank book after breakfast. Also, some papers with Dix's signature. In case you need to draw any money out, you'll have to practice Dix's signature. Darn it, I mean your signature. Now how did I forget that?"

"Do you find it so hard to remember?" he smiled.

"Mostly, your name comes easier than you might think."

When breakfast was finished, he reached for his Durham and papers; she took them from his hand and rolled one for herself as well. He made no comment, taking her actions as a customary thing to do. Lucia, the breed girl, appeared and started to clear away the dishes.

Sabina said, "Lucia, this is my husband, returned after a long absence."

The girl dropped him a sort of curtsey. "Eet is good you are returnin', Señor Ryder. I make the welcome to you."

"*Gracias,* Lucia," Ryder smiled. "Thank you very much."

Sabina gave the girl directions for clearing up the Señor Ryder's bedroom, speaking fluent Spanish. The girl nodded and disappeared

"Did she cook this breakfast, or did you?" Dix Ryder asked.

"I did. You'll remember, you always wanted to have breakfast with me, alone, so I let her sleep late. After all, she cooks supper — sometimes Flapjack does it — and then clears away later —"

"Yes, I suddenly remember now," Ryder smiled.

"There'll be a lot of things to remember, Dix."

"Yes, Sabina," he said meekly.

She left the table to get the bank book, returning with pen, ink and various papers. "You'll find Dix Ryder's signature on those papers. Please practice it."

She left to give directions to Lucia in the kitchen, returning in about fifteen minutes to find the name "Dixon Ryder," written numerous times on a sheet of paper. "It's not too difficult," he told her, as she scrutinized the sheet. "The writing is much like mine. Once I got into the swing of the curves and the way the 'i' was dotted —"

"Why," she exclaimed, "there's so little difference —"

"Anyway," he pointed out, "a man's handwriting can change a heap in five years. I reckon there'll be no trouble at the bank."

She agreed, then a small frown appeared between her eyes. "There's just one thing troubling me," she admitted.

"What's that?"

"How are we going to explain your absence for five years — an explanation that will stand up?"

"I figured that out this morning when I woke up."

"But where have you been?"

"In Mexico — doing secret work for the government."

"I don't understand."

"I'll explain. After the Civil War there was a faction in Congress that wanted an excuse to declare war on Mexico. They've been working in that direction for a long, long time. The President was aware of the plan and wanted to break it up. I was chosen to go to Mexico and run down certain renegade citizens of this country who were working for the scoundrels in Congress and see that they were arrested. It was a long job. In case anybody down there happened to recognize me as Dix Ryder, the news was given out that Dix Ryder was dead. You were in on the secret and you can pretend that you heard from me every so often. Now that the plot has been destroyed, I'm back."

She looked doubtful. "Do you think that will stand up?"

"Who's to prove it isn't true?" he said. "I'll admit it sounds sort of fake-like, but it would take some time for anybody to dig out that it wasn't so. You can always say I had a relation close to the President, and I figure to have things settled hereabouts before anyone has time to dig out the truth."

"Maybe it will work," she half smiled. "Anyway, we can try."

"Fine. Later I want to ride into Arboledo and see how well you've taught me my lesson, but I'm going to the bunkhouse first." He got to his feet, found his gun and strapped it about his hips, donned the black sombrero. "S'long. See you later, Sabina."

"Get home early, Dix," she smiled.

He left by the kitchen and crossed the patio, heading toward the bunkhouse. Pete Gratton and Jeff Clayton greeted him with "Mawnin', Dix." Flapjack Hannan was in his kitchen from whence came the clatter of dishes being washed. Amber Odell and Dusty Rhodes greeted Dix respectfully.

Clayton said, "We didn't get started, 'cause I didn't know what orders you might have to give."

"I'd hoped you wouldn't, Jeff," Dix nodded. "I'd like for you to accompany me to town today. Pete," — to Gratton — "you're boss in Jeff's absence. I understand our cows are pretty much scattered. You take Amber and Dusty and start gathering them in, nearer the house, and stream. You can make a start anyway."

The men nodded. Odell said, "We already got the hawsses saddled, just awaitin' orders."

"Good. Saddle up for me, too, will you?"

Amber said, "I'll do that. Look, Mr. Ryder —"

"I think I told you to address me as Dix, Amber."

"Yessir, Dix. Look here, I got a likely looking pony picked out for you, figuring that horse you rode in on deserved a rest."

"A fine idea. Thanks." To Dusty, "Drift over and tell Flapjack to get a buckboard hitched. He's coming to town with Jeff and me. Tell him to make out a list of supplies he needs."

Dusty Rhodes nodded and disappeared through the doorway. In a few minutes he was back. "Flapjack is already started hitchin'. He says he don't need to make out no list. He's plumb out of everything and can order from memory."

Dix Ryder laughed. "I hope he's got a long memory, because I figure there's a lot been needed while I been away."

Odell, Pete Gratton, and Dusty Rhodes were already leaving, and a short time later the hoofbeats of their departing ponies could be heard.

"Some crew," Jeff Clayton sighed, "and all there is to be done."

"Quit fretting about it," Ryder said. "I've been thinking about that. Got a note written out that I want you to telegraph from the T.N. & A.S. depot. If we don't get some hands in short order, I'll be damn' surprised. Let's get started."

Flapjack Hannan was already in the seat of the buckboard when Clayton and Ryder appeared. Dix answered his morning greeting, saying, "Jeff and I will go on ahead, Flapjack. You can catch up with us in town." When he saw that Hannan looked dubious, he asked, "Anything wrong with that idea?"

"Not from your standpoint," the old

cook replied, "I just hope I meet you all right."

"Why not?" Ryder asked.

"We—ell," Hannan said hesitatingly, "every time I hit Arboledo, some of them Wickmann plug-uglies sort of get to making it tough on me. Once they dumped all my supplies outten my wagon —"

Dix Ryder considered. "Hmm. This Wickmann must have got himself quite a gang."

"Most of 'em —" Hannan spat an expletive with a long stream of tobacco juice from the seat of the buckboard, "is just hangers-on, tryin' to get on Wickmann's payroll, I figure, thinkin' he's the big boss hereabouts. Then he's got some punchers hit town, ever' so often — leastwise they look like waddies, but I don't know where they work. No outfit 'round here hires 'em. They jest come and go, seems like."

"Don't let it worry you. You'll meet us in town. See you there."

He and Clayton swung up into saddles and took off at an easy lope, while Hannan and the buckboard came more slowly at the rear. A mile from the house, Clayton asked, "How's that new bronc Odell picked for you?"

"Seems like a right nice horse, Jeff.

Responds at the slightest touch, nice easy gait. Let's try some speed."

The animals picked up the pace. The scenery flashed past along the trail, until cactus, mesquite, grass became a blur. The two men slowed at the river and reined in while the animals drank. Clayton looked at the horse, a gray gelding. "Still like your mount?"

"He's all right. Odell has a good eye. Think I'll ride him for a spell and give my own mount a rest —"

"That is your own mount, Dix," Clayton said meaningly.

Ryder laughed. "That's good, Jeff. Check me up every time I make a mistake. That's one reason I wanted you with me, today, so you can sort of clue me if I'm uncertain about anyone we meet."

"I figured as much, Dix."

"By the way —" the horses were mounting the opposite bank of the stream by this time and moving at a slower pace again — "how's the DR fixed for horse flesh?"

"That's the one thing we do have. Horses. We used to have a right smart *remuda* — you always insisted on that, remember? — and we still have a good-sized bunch; most of 'em just eating their heads off and running up bills for feed at times when the grass is scanty some months. You thinking of mounts for more men? I just don't know where —"

"I've got that figured out too. I got a message I want you to telegraph from the station, like I said. Here, read it."

The horses slowed to a walk while Ryder passed over a sheet of paper. It was addressed to somebody named Matthew Kimball, at a Texas town Clayton knew to be near the Monarch Ranch. He frowned as he scanned the words:

Dear Matt: If you're not afraid of a scrap, with work attached, gather up as many hands as you can and come on to Arboledo, Arizona, plenty pronto. Horses here. Ask for

Santone Austin

Clayton looked somewhat bewildered. "Well, this sounds fine, up to a point, but, hell, Dix, you can't sign that Austin name. You'll give the whole game away."

"If I signed it 'Dix Ryder,' they wouldn't know who Dix Ryder is. How about the station man at the depot? Is he likely to talk?"

"I don't reckon so. Never knew him to

discuss anybody's telegrams. And I know he don't like the Wickmann bunch. Still and all, it might be risky —"

"Exactly why it has to be signed Austin, Jeff. Now, here's what you do. At the depot you say that you took on a new hand, named Austin, and this Austin said he knew some friends who needed jobs. So you've sent for them to come. That sounds natural." He added, "Might be a bit risky, too, inasmuch as it tips our hand off, in a way."

For a moment Clayton's face looked grim. "Risky, all right, but I'll do it, Dix. You're the boss. Mebbe we can get away with it. Think this Kimball hombre will get anybody to come?"

Dix Ryder grinned. "You wait and see. It'll be up to you to meet him when they arrive. Get 'em alone and then explain things, and tell you were told I'd kick the slats out of any man who didn't remember to call me Dix. They'll be grabbing the first train out of town, I figure. You're going to have some trains to meet, after tomorrow, and then hustle 'em out of town as fast as possible. If Matt doesn't arrive with a bunch of fighting cow-pokes I'll eat my Stet-hat."

"I'd hate to see you have to do that,"

Clayton laughed.

"Now, here's something else, Jeff." Ryder told Clayton of the talk he'd had with Sabina and the alibi they were to use to explain the five years' absence.

"I think it might work," Clayton nodded seriously. "And who's to prove otherwise? I remember when that ruckus broke out down in Mexico, readin' about it in the paper. It said the U.S. Government had been working on the deal for years and had a lot of — I think they were called under-cover men — cleaning out and arresting a bunch of skunks. Anything else you should tell me?"

"I practiced the signature for the bank, in case it becomes necessary to draw from the Ryder account. I'm sure my writing will pass."

"I don't figure there'll be any doubt, once they've seen you, Dix, particularly if you plan to deposit some money today."

"I do. And that reminds me. What bills are owing to men around town."

"Hmmm . . . lemme see. The General Store has money coming, likewise the feed store. There's some wages due the boys too, but those can wait —"

"T'hell they can!" Dix snapped. "You figure what's due everybody, including yourself, and I'll pay those back wages when we get back home tonight. Like's not, while we're in town, you'll think of some supplies we need, in addition to what Hannan needs."

"We—ell, that's true," Clayton nodded seriously. "We could use a couple of new brandin' irons from the blacksmith shop in town. We used to have our own blacksmith, as you'll remember, Dix, but now — oh, yes, the buckboard needs a new set of harness. Flapjack's been repairing it with haywire, until I'm not certain whether there's more wire than leather. And then —"

"Get what's needed, Jeff."

Ahead they could now sight the first buildings of Arboledo, bathed in morning sunlight. A few fleecy clouds floated in a sapphire sky, and a slight breeze lifted across the range. They crossed a plank bridge, at the edge of town, joining either bank of the Sangriento River, which they crossed previously when leaving the DR holdings. River? More like a wide stream, heading back in the Sangriento Mountains, until it crossed Arboledo's Main Street, coursed under another bridge at the T.N. & A.S. rails and then continued its shallow flow until it finally sank out of sight in semi-desert country, some ten miles farther on.

Scattered about here were a handful of Mexican blocky adobe buildings, and some tall cottonwoods. Nearly naked Mexican children played in the sun; a bunch of chickens pecked futilely at the sandy soil. The two men pulled their horses to a halt beneath a tall cottonwood's shade, to await Flapjack Hannan's arrival with the buckboard. The children gathered about them a minute or so, eyeing them curiously, and then returned to their play, making the air shrill with their cries.

Clayton rolled a cigarette and lighted it. "I've often wondered Dix," he commented, through a puff of gray smoke, "why kids have to scream and yell so much when they play."

Dix Ryder chuckled. "Reckon they're developing their lungs — just as you and I did, once. It's part of their growing —"

Clayton interrupted, "On your guard, Dix! Here comes Finch Orcutt. Now, don't forget —"

"Orcutt? Oh, yeah, Finch Orcutt. Town marshal. Used to run the General Store. Good friend of mine. I got it."

He watched the man approaching along the street on a brown horse. A tall, spare man with wide shoulders, prominent jaw-bones and a "horse-tail" mustache.

Well, Dix thought, swiftly gathering all the details he could summon, here comes the first test. Sure hope I can get away with it.

Chapter IX

Even before Orcutt had drawn near, Dix suddenly lifted his voice in a wild yell of greeting, the abrupt blast halting the noise of shrieking children.

"Finch, you woolly old coyote! Heard you was still cheating the undertaker, but had taken on some law-enforcing job."

"Yeah. You blasted gay-cat! Gawd, it's good to see you again."

Orcutt loped up and pulled to a quick halt alongside Ryder's horse. The men shook hands, Orcutt saying, "Always felt you'd be back. Never did believe you were dead, no more than Sabina did."

Questions and answers flew between the two men. "Heard yesterday you were back. Didn't believe it until Porky Sullivan said it was you. Figured to ride out and see you last night — was on my way now — but figured I better not intrude your first night home. Bet Sabina was glad —" He broke off to say hello to Clayton.

"Hell's bells! You know you're welcome any time." Dix indicated the narrow, curved-end badge on Orcutt's shirt. "How come you got into that game?"

"Never did take much to peddlin' vittles to folks, so when I got a good offer for my store, I took it. Things was gettin' sort of rough in town, so I decided I'd do my part. I run for marshal and got it."

"Got things quieted down, Finch?"

"Ain't so bad in town. I ain't finicky 'bout makin' arrests when necessary, but it keeps me right busy. Wickmann has quite a following — you heard he was back, I reckon."

Dix nodded grimly. "Yeah. And I'm aiming to do something about it. You just handle the town, Finch, and I'll see what I can do in other directions —"

"But where in hell you been, Dix?"

Ryder frowned slightly. "That's a long story, Finch. I'll tell you when I've got more time. Briefly, I had to pretend to be dead while I did some secret work for the U.S. Government, down in Mexico. But it was all sort of hush-hush stuff —"

"Right, Dix. I won't tell a soul —"

"That's okay. Now that the work is done, I don't much care who knows, so don't feel you got to go around with a gag in your mouth — oh, here comes Flapjack now. We've been waiting for him to show up."

125

A look of relief crossed the old cook's features when he saw Dix and Clayton waiting for him. He whipped his team into a faster gait and soon pulled alongside as he slowed down.

"What's your first stop, Flapjack?" Ryder asked.

"Daniel's Gin'ral Store," Hannan replied.

"That's my old place," Orcutt commented. "Best in Arboledo."

They reined the horses in beside the wagon and headed along Main Street, Finch Orcutt still talking, telling Ryder of the changes in town during his absence. Unbeknownst to Orcutt, all such information was welcome to Ryder, serving in place of one more lesson in the things he should know. ". . . and we got a new man runnin' the gun shop, now," Orcutt was saying. "Old Webb Jones finally kicked the bucket. There's a new hotel opened, while you was away — Cowman's Cottage. It's a flea bag if I ever saw one." He scowled. "Now, mebbe, you're back, you can talk the town into buildin' a new jail, too. I been tryin' for some time to get one."

"I'll do what I can," Ryder nodded. "Got things to do today. Hope they won't take too long. Yeah, Finch, I can see Arboledo has grown a lot since I've been away. It's damn good to be back."

They were nearing the center of town by now. He heard someone yell, "There's Dix Ryder!" Inwardly Dix groaned and braced himself.

Other men took up the cry. They seemed to be approaching from all directions, smiling faces to welcome him home. The horse and wagon couldn't make any progress against the numbers gathering around them. Dix was forced to brush off the questions hurled at him, as to where he'd been. He reached down and grasped the hands of men he was supposed to know. And all the time he was compelled to maintain a mask of sheer delight in the greetings.

Finally Orcutt broke in, "All right, fellows, break it up. You can realize that Dix has a lot to do in town today. Let's give him a chance to get on with his business. He'll see you all later."

Ryder shot him a grateful glance as the crowd began to disperse. Finally, horses and men moved on. Ryder said, "Looks like we got a lot of friends on our side."

Clayton said, "Yeah, but they're all afraid of Wickmann, too."

"That's the truth," Orcutt agreed. "We

need you to organize folks, Dix. I can see you've heard about Wickmann. You ran him out of town, remember. He's back, but it's a dangerous Wickmann now. Lot different from what he used to be. How do you figure to handle him?"

"You tell me and I'll tell you," Ryder laughed shortly. "I'll cross that river when I come to it."

There was an almost unbroken line of hitch-racks along the street in front of the various buildings of commercial enterprise. Just beyond the corner of Main and Bisbee Streets, Hannan turned the team and buckboard in to a tierail before Daniels' General Store. Ryder and Jeff Clayton left their horses and stepped to the ground. Orcutt stayed in his saddle, saying, "I'll see you later, Dix."

"Come out to the house and set a spell, Finch, when you get a chance," Ryder invited. "Sabina'll be glad to see you too. We can spin some windies about the old days and see who's the biggest liar."

Orcutt rode on toward the livery stable. On the sidewalk, Ryder said, "Flapjack, you go on in and buy what's needed. Have Daniels tote up what's owing to him. Tell him I'll be there in a short spell and give him what's due. Jeff, you said you had some things to get. I want to go to the bank. I'll meet you both here inside an hour or so. Okay?"

Clayton said, "Don't you want me to go with you?"

"I'll make out, providing the bank's in the same building."

"Still a couple doors from this General Store like always."

"Thanks. I thought it might have moved."

The men parted. A woman carrying a sun parasol, in long skirts that kicked up the dust at her heels, nodded to Dix. He touched the brim of his sombrero in return, having no idea who she was.

Ryder turned into the bank, a one-story building of brick and timbers, with the wide entrance between two windows. "Let me see," was the thought running through his mind. "The cashier's name is Willie Roberts — gray hair — glasses — skinny."

A long wall ran along one side of the interior, broken by two grilled windows. At the other wall was a flat-topped desk for the convenience of customers. At the rear was a door marked PRIVATE. That would lead to Banker Phelps' office. Charlie Phelps.

Ryder crossed the floor to the first

grilled window. Laughing, he said, "Damned if it isn't Willie Roberts. And you don't look a day older."

The man looked up, peered through rimless glasses, then a wide smile crossed his face. "Dix Ryder, by all that's holy! I'm delighted to see you're back, Mr. Ryder. Somebody told me you rode into town yesterday, but I didn't know where you'd been —"

"Look here, Willie, I'm busy as a one-armed brand man with fleas. You'll get the story later. Meanwhile, I want to deposit some money. Here's the bank book." From his pockets he began to produce gold coins and rumpled bills to build a heap of cash on the counter in front of Roberts.

"Yessir, Mr. Ryder. You want to put this all in?"

"Leave me about three hundred. I've got some bills to pay around town." The transaction was completed quickly, the money counted and entered in the bank book which was returned to Ryder along with the money he was retaining. He said, "Thanks, Willie. Is Charlie in?"

"He's in his office, Mr. Ryder."

"Ryder strode to the door marked PRIVATE and without ceremony pushed open the door and entered. Inside the room, a portly individual with gray hair and sideburns sat at a roll-top desk, scrutinizing a ledger, and mumbling to himself. At his elbow stood a bottle of whisky and a half-finished tumbler. At the sound of Ryder's entry, he swung around in his chair, and said irritatedly, "Now, look here, young man, most folks are polite enough to knock — yes, polite enough to knock, before —"

Ryder swung the door to behind him, laughing, "Charlie, you old rotgut guzzler, have you forgotten your old friend?"

Phelps squinted at Ryder, then his eyes widened, his jaw dropped. "So it's so, so it's so. You *are* back! Heard a rumor to that effect — yes, heard a rumor. Never believed it, no, never believed it —" as he got cumbersomely out of his chair, one fat hand extended.

Ryder took it in his hand, gripped it hard. "Everything looks about the same. The town has grown some —"

"Growing in leaps and bounds, yes, leaps and bounds. Well, drag up a chair. Here —" bustling about like a fat old woman, to push Ryder into a chair. "Got another glass around here, some place, yes, got another glass."

He talked continually, repeating phrases,

as he found a glass and poured whisky into it. "Sit down, sit down. Tell me where you've been."

To avoid answering at once, Ryder busied himself with the drink. He set it down a moment at the edge of the desk. "Still, a good judge of liquor, Charlie; I can't fault you any on your taste."

Phelps nodded. "Hard to beat old James E. Pepper, I always say — Pepper hard to beat. But where you been — where you been?"

"It's a long story, Charlie, and I haven't time now. Got a lot to do trying to get things settled. I'll be in again. Meanwhile, Sabina said something about you letting her have some money one time when she was sort of strapped —"

"Nothing to it, Dix. A few measly dollars, yes, a few measly dollars. Didn't even enter it in the books." Ryder pressed him for the amount and he finally gave it. Ryder reached in his pocket and repaid the loan. Phelps continued, "Liked to have made her a loan on the DR — yes, on the DR. But the way conditions were, I didn't dare risk it, didn't dare risk it. Bad banking principles, y'know, under conditions —"

"Conditions?"

"Feller here now. Wickmann's name, yes,

Wickmann. I don't think he's to be trusted, not to be trusted. I refused to handle his account. But he's costing my bank money, yes, costing us money. He'll lend to everybody at high interest, very high interest. Got half the people in this country in his debt, I dare say. Then, he's quick to foreclose, quick to foreclose. Fools borrow from him instead of coming here. Got a bad crowd under his thumb here, too, yes, a bad crowd."

It was with difficulty Ryder managed to escape, and then only when he'd promised to "come in, again, soon."

On the street once more, he headed toward Porky Sullivan's bar. When he entered, Porky glanced around and a smile curved his lips. He gave Ryder a quick wink, and then set out a bottle of beer and a box of cigars and tumbler, with a "Glad to see you in, again, Dix."

There were only three men drinking at the bar. Ryder wondered if he should know them. Porky caught his thought, and shook his head, commenting, "Lots of new-comers here, since you left, Dix." So that was taken care of. Within a few minutes the three men finished their drinks and departed. Now, Ryder was the sole customer.

"You don't know how glad I was, Dix," Porky grinned, "when Pete Gratton rode in last night with the news you were going to carry the bluff through."

"If I can," Ryder replied dubiously. "I'm always afraid of making a slip, and —"

"Forget it — you'll get by. Figured out a way to explain your absence, yet?"

Ryder told him of the alibi he'd concocted. "You might let something like that get rumored around, Porky. Let on it was all very secret and so on."

Porky agreed. "I can always make out that I don't know too much myself."

"That's the ticket. Now tell me what you can about this Wickmann who seems to have this whole range buffaloed."

"That goddamn Wickmann!" Porky spat. "He's got a following made up of the scum of the town. Finch Orcutt is always having to arrest some hoodlum, but it don't do much good." Ryder asked for particulars. Porky explained, "We got a gutless Justice of the Peace here — reg'lar old goat who's afraid of offending somebody. Orcutt will bring a scut up before the JP and the worst the feller gets is a five buck fine for disturbin' the peace. And Wickmann is allus on hand to pay the fine. The rough element figures to get away with anything, knowin' that Wickmann will take care of 'em."

Porky talked steadily for ten minutes. More and more it appeared where skulduggery was afoot, Wickmann was at the bottom of it.

"He's a stronger man than he was five years ago when you run him out, Dix, but I still figure you can do it again. I'm hoping so —" He broke off suddenly, as the bat-wing doors of the saloon parted. "Brace yourself, Dix. Here comes Wickmann, now."

Chapter X

Dix Ryder didn't turn at the sounds of footsteps arriving. That was unnecessary, as he could view Wickmann's approach in the back-bar mirror, beyond Porky's stacked pyramids of gleaming glasses. Yes, was the thought that ran swiftly through Ryder's mind, this hombre must have changed. He may have been just a no-good thug five years ago, but now he could be dangerous, dangerous combined with a certain cunning.

He continued to sip at his glass of beer. Wickmann took a stance at the bar and ordered a "shot." Porky set it out. Wickmann tossed off the whisky at a gulp, tossed money on the bar and then pretended to start out. Abruptly, he turned back, saying, "Porky, there's a rumor around town that Dix Ryder is back. Of course, that's impossible, but have you heard — ?"

Ryder lifted his head and looked at Wickmann, full face. "Yeah, Wickmann, I'm back," he said coldly, "so it's not impossible."

For a moment, Wickmann just stared as though doubting the evidence of his eyes. His mouth dropped open; he swallowed hard. He brushed one hand across his eyes, as though trying to clear his vision. His face turned ashen and he recoiled a step.

"My God!" he blurted involuntarily. "It *is* you!"

"You know of any reason it shouldn't be?" Dix snapped.

"But — but you're dead," Wickmann stammered.

Dix smiled thinly. "I heard there was talk to that effect —"

"But you can't be Dix Ryder —" Wickmann began, then checked the words. He forced a sickly smile. "But I — I reckon you are," he concluded lamely. Swiftly gathering his jumbled wits, he thrust out one hand. "God, it's good to see you, Dix."

Ryder ignored the proffered hand, as he reached for a cigar from the box Porky had placed on the bar. He bit off one end, scratched a match, and lighted the smoke.

"Good to see me back?" Ryder said caustically. "Now you know you don't mean that for truth, Wickmann. Why lie about it?" His gaze flitted swiftly over Wickmann's form, not missing the bulge in the man's long coat, beneath one shoulder, where an under-arm gun reposed in holster.

Wickmann stiffened a little. "So you're aiming to hold our old trouble against me," he exclaimed.

"I know of no reason I shouldn't," Ryder snapped.

"But — but that was five years ago —" he protested.

"From all I hear you haven't changed any."

"I don't know what you've heard, but it's all lies, Ryder. Sure, I know I've made enemies. Lots of folks don't like me. They can't understand I've changed a heap in the last five years, saw the error of my ways. I'll admit I was pretty wild once, but I'm a reformed man, you might say."

"I'll say it when I believe it," Ryder said tersely.

Wickmann shrugged. "All right, if you see it that way. I was hoping to be friends. Just what you aiming to do about it?"

"Give you a chance to be honest," Ryder said bluntly. "I don't like you, and I don't like anyone who does. I ran you out of town once, and I reckon I can do it again, if it becomes necessary. You go along and run your business on the level, and we won't have any trouble. But you make just one bad move and your sit-spot's going to be in a sling — if not worse. Now it's up to you to say what you're going to do about it. Mr. Sam Colt offers a way of settling arguments, if you don't like what I've said."

It was the challenge direct, but Wickmann lacked the courage to back up the thought that crossed his mind. He drew back and said, somewhat shakily, "Oh, no, Ryder. I know your rep with a six-shooter. That way isn't for me. The West has become civilized, I'm glad to see, and the day of settling arguments with hot lead —"

"Oh, hell," Ryder said impatiently, "enough of that palavering."

Wickmann gulped hard. "But what can I do to prove I want to be friends?"

"You don't want to be friends and you know it goddamn well. Wickmann, the DR has lost a lot of cows. I want it stopped."

"If there's cow thievin' going on, I've had nothing to do with it. The Apaches have been right busy —"

"That's a lot of cow-chips too," Ryder snapped. "Three DR hands have been ambushed and shot. An Apache lance was run through one, as well. Now you know dam' well no Indian is going off and leave without his lance, when his victim is already dead. Two of the hands had Apache arrows stuck in 'em. I've talked to Jeff Clayton who saw the bodies. Those arrows were just stuck under the skin, not in deep like they should have been if they'd been shot from a bow. Pretty clumsy work, if you ask me. You'll have to think better than that, Wickmann."

"I'll swear I had nothing to do with it."

"Can you swear it wasn't done by your orders?"

" 'Course — 'course, I can." Wickmann was perspiring freely. He removed his sombrero and mopped his forehead with a bandanna. "As — as for the DR missing cows, if the Injuns wa'n't to blame, mebbe the critters just strayed off. I've heard you didn't have enough of a crew out there to take care of things proper."

"Where'd you get your information? From Hugo Ridge?"

Wickmann's eyes evaded Ryder's steely glance. "Don't rightly remember where I heard it," he stated.

"Well, that will be corrected right *pronto*," Ryder said coldly. "And I'm giving orders that if you, or any of your followers show up on DR holdings, they're to be plugged. So take warning — now!"

"But — but — I ain't got no followers."

"I hear differently."

Wickmann began to back away. "Well, I'm sorry to see you don't want to be friendly, but I promise you'll have no trouble on my account."

Ryder laughed sarcastically and turned back to the bar. Visibly shaken, Wickmann backed to the swinging doors, then in a sudden frantic haste he left the barroom and stepped into the street.

On the way back to his own place, Wickmann saw Alonzo Tidwell riding into town, and he hailed him. Tidwell pulled into the sidewalk. "Just comin' in to see you, Purdy. You forgot to write out that bill-of-sale you promised to give Hugo last night. He'd like to get it."

"Cows ready to move?" Wickmann asked quickly.

"Will be in another day or so."

Wickmann swore. "Finished branding the new brands?"

"Got around fifty yet to do."

"You ride back to Hugo fast as horse flesh will carry you. I want them fifty that's untouched thronged back on DR land — you can ride in again for that bill-of-sale. I want those other steers pushed over the line as fast as possible —"

"But — but," Tidwell frowned. "You

mean you're turning that fifty, with untouched brands, back to the DR? What for?"

"Don't ask so many damn' questions, 'Lonzo," Wickmann snapped irritatedly.

Tidwell said shrewdly, "You sound like you might have had a run-in with Dix Ryder. You gone scared?"

Wickmann got better control of himself. "Certainly, I'm not scared. Yes, I saw Ryder. It's just that I want them branded cows got out of the country as fast as possible, and then get my hands in town. I've got to play the game different from now on. And warn the boys not to be caught on DR holdings. This Ryder is just aching for trouble, and I'm not ready for it yet. I've got to figure a way to outfox him."

"You convinced now he's the real Dix Ryder?"

"Sure looks, acts, and talks like the Ryder of five years back. But I don't see how —" Wickmann broke off. "Dammit, 'Lonzo, we're wasting time. You get back out to Ridge soon's possible, even if you kill a horse gettin' there. Move, goddamit!"

Chapter XI

Ryder gave a soft laugh as the swinging doors of the saloon closed behind the departing Wickmann. He glanced at Porky. The fat bartender was grinning widely.

"The house buys you a fresh bottle of beer on that one, Dix. Or do you want a shot? You handled that neat. Wickmann looked sort of shook-up, if you ask me. Him and his slimey ways."

"I hope he's shook-up," Ryder replied. "Beer, thanks, Porky."

The two men talked while Ryder's cigar smoke curled above the bar, and while Porky was at his everlasting polishing of glasses. Porky mentioned certain names and occupations of men around town, men Ryder was supposed to know, even though slightly. Ryder committed the details to memory. Finishing his beer, Ryder took his departure.

He strolled down one side of the street and back the other, being stopped every so often by "an old friend." It kept his brain working fast in each instance to place such people, though in some cases names popped in his memory the instant he was approached. He settled a long-standing bill at the hay and feed store and another at the livery stable, each stop requiring longer time than he cared to give. Mostly he was obliged to give evasive replies to probing questions. At the harness and saddle shop he learned that Jeff Clayton had left some time ago.

Passing a restaurant, new since his supposed disappearance of five years ago, Ryder decided he was hungry again, and stopped long enough to stow away a cup of coffee and a cold beef sandwich. The street was hot in the noonday sun, throwing black shadows between buildings. There were more wagons and ponies waiting at the hitch-racks now. Finally, he turned back toward the general store where he had left Flapjack, thinking to find Clayton waiting there.

As he approached the store he heard a crowd of people yelling and laughing. Ryder pushed through a bunch of jeering men just in time to see Flapjack Hannan down on all fours, trying to retrieve a number of spilled packages of groceries the cook had been buying. Ryder glanced quickly over the crowd. An unshaven, unwashed crowd, down-at-the-heel hood-lums, most of them appeared to be.

Ryder moved to the center of the group into the cleared space, helped Hannan up, then assisted him to retrieve the packages and place them in the wagon, where other sacks and bundles had already been unloaded.

Hannan had finally found his voice. "Gawd! Am I glad to see you, Dix," he panted.

"Never mind that," Ryder said grimly. "Who did it?"

"Ain't — ain't certain," Hannan replied. "Somebody tripped me. That's the second time since I've been here."

He waited by the wagon while Ryder rounded the hitch-rack and faced the gang of hoodlums. "All right, who's the smart aleck among you bunch of mangy coy-otes?"

Somebody yelled, "That's Dix Ryder!" Some of the crowd began to melt away. The majority stayed, however.

A man yelled, "Don't let him bluff you, boys!"

It was Doag Barbe, his red beard bris-tling angrily. He pushed up to within a few feet of Ryder. "I don't say I done it, but if I did, what's it to you?" he snarled.

145

"Just this," Ryder snapped. His hand lifted with the speed of a striking rattler and he slammed it, back-handed, across Barbe's face.

Barbe's head jerked back, and he staggered a couple of steps before righting himself. Red angry glints showed in his eyes, as he stood glaring at Ryder.

"Now," Ryder told him, "if you want more, jerk that iron you're wearing and get to work." He hadn't made a move with his own gun — yet.

Barbe shook his head. "I ain't fool enough to buck you with guns, but I'll square this — you'll see."

He turned away as though to depart, and then wheeled and came back with a rush, a bunched right hand swinging from down near his hip in what was intended for a knockout blow.

Ryder hadn't been fooled a moment by the clumsy maneuver. He stepped out of line just before the blow landed, then hammered a hard left into Barbe's middle.

An explosive grunt was expelled from Barbe's lips as he bent suddenly forward — just in time for his whiskered chin to meet Ryder's slashing right fist. The blow didn't travel far, but it seemed to lift Barbe completely from his feet before he went crashing to the sidewalk, his hat flying off.

A wild yell of delight left Flapjack Hannan's lips. One or two other bystanders cheered. The Barbe gang looked disgruntled. From down the street came yells of "Fight! Fight!" Men were running to see the action.

Barbe rolled completely over, once, then got to hands and knees, groggily shaking his head. His eyes looked glazed. Ryder watched him narrowly.

Gradually the man's vision seemed to clear; then he raised to knees and his right hand swept to gun holster.

Ryder laughed contemptuously as his own gun came out. Closing in swiftly, he brought the barrel of the Colt's .44 sharply across the side of Barbe's head. Barbe's gun barrel didn't even have time to clear his holster. For a moment he seemed to stiffen, then abruptly he dived forward on his face to lie still.

"Not worth wasting a cartridge on," Ryder smiled around the crowd. "Well, who's next?"

No one answered. The crowd was backing away now.

Again that contemptuous laugh parted Ryder's lips. "What? None of you lousy, two-bit, gall-sored hyenas got enough guts to take up your pard's fight? Come on, wake up! Show me you got some nerve anyway. What? Not one of you? Any two of you, then. Or three. All right, you skunks name it."

Somebody yelled, "That's the old Dix Ryder!"

Flapjack Hannan was yelling and hooting like a madman. It seemed no one wanted any part of Ryder's game. Some one started more cheering. Barbe's gang of hoodlums seemed more than willing to get away now, as they slunk off in all directions, leaving the unconscious Barbe stretched on the sidewalk.

"Nice work, Dix." It was Jeff Clayton.

"You saw it?" And when Clayton nodded, Ryder said, "Not much of a fracas."

"It'll make a few people think, anyway. I was staying back, just to see if any of those other thugs jumped in to help Barbe. The scut got just what he deserved."

Finch Orcutt came running up. He glanced at Ryder, then at the red-bearded form sprawled on the sidewalk. "What happened? I was way the other side of town when I heard yells of 'Fight!' Came on as fast as I could get here." Ryder explained matters.

Orcutt said, "You want to make charges against him, Dix?"

Ryder laughed and shook his head. "Far's I'm concerned, he can run loose. Maybe he'll feel like trying again."

"I doubt it — not in the same way. I just figger I'll toss him in the hoosegow anyway for disturbin' the peace." He studied the unconscious form. "Just how am I suppose to get him to the jail? He can't walk, and he's too big to drag all that way. Mebbe we can get him to his feet." He turned to the men standing about. "If somebody will please bring a bucket of water —"

That was as far as he got. There were sudden hoots of laughter and half a dozen men dashed into stores to return in a few minutes with brimming pails of water to dash over Barbe. Buckets emptied, they hurried back to fill them again. The laughter increased. A small pool of water began to form about the stunned Barbe. Consciousness was returning and he began to move arms and legs as though he were swimming. Finally, he managed to rise to hands and knees, only to be knocked flat again when a fresh deluge splashed over him.

The man was still groggy when Orcutt jerked him to his feet and started Barbe's stumbling steps in the direction of the town jail.

Once more the street resumed normal procedure. Ryder asked, "Did you send that telegram, Jeff?"

Clayton nodded. "The clerk at the depot didn't ask any questions so I didn't have anything to explain. Then I sort of sashayed around town, talking to folks about you."

"What about me?"

"Oh, I was just explaining to folks that you'd be right busy for a spell and wouldn't have much time to sit and chew the rag. Thought it might avoid some awkward questions when you meet people."

"Thanks. Good idea, Jeff. Had your dinner?"

"I grabbed me a quick bite at a restaurant. Figured you'd do the same. I got that new harness and some other stuff. They're in the wagon."

Ryder nodded, then turned to Hannan who had dismounted from the wagon to join them. He was still cackling. "Hee! hee! I wouldn't missed thet fight for a millyun dollars. Thet Doag Barbe has needed his comeuppance for some long time, now. I reckon you showed him, Dix, it don't pay to monkey with us DR men."

"We'll keep trying to convince such scuts," Ryder said gravely, "that we intend to keep the pressure on, too. Flapjack, you catch any dinner yet?"

"Got me a bait in the store while Daniels was making out our order — b'iled ham and pickles and crackers and some sardines and jam and canned tomatoes and peaches and a tin o' corned beef and a can o' beans —"

"Just a little snack to hold you over until supper," Ryder said dryly. "Too bad you didn't think to get some cheese, too. Your order filled yet?"

"There's just a few sacks and sech to be toted out yet. And I told Daniels you'd be in to settle the bill and he said there wartn't no hurry, but he'd total it up."

"Let's go in and settle it then. Then we'll head back home."

It didn't occur to him until afterward how easily the word "home" had come to his lips.

He said to Clayton, "Oh, yes, I saw Wickmann." He told of seeing the man in Porky Sullivan's. Clayton looked concerned. "He looked sort of shocked when he saw me. Tried to be friendly, but I didn't go for it."

Clayton spat. "I'd figure when he's

acting friendly he is most dangerous. Likely just pretending, until he can figure out some more of his skulduggery."

"If so," Ryder said cheerfully, "I think we can handle anything he might scheme up, Jeff, so don't fret about it a minute. There's going to be a new deal around here. Arboledo isn't any place for crooks to run loose, and I'm going to make them understand just that."

Chapter XII

Five days slipped past, with Santone Austin ably filling the position of Dix Ryder — so far as concerns running the crew. Jeff Clayton was spending most of his time in Arboledo, awaiting the train that might be depositing the cow-punchers Dix had telegraphed for. Under Ryder's continual drive, the DR cows were being gathered and bunched nearer the ranch house and spread along the stream. He was considerably irked that faster progress couldn't be made, even though he was so short-handed with only Dusty Rhodes, Pete Gratton and Amber Odell to help.

He had made two swift rides, to Arboledo and back, to size up the situation. There'd been no more trouble with the Wickmann crowd. Doag Barbe had been brought before the spineless Justice of the Peace, so Finch Orcutt related disgustedly, and been fined five dollars for disturbing the peace — nothing more. Wickmann was on hand promptly to pay the fine, and though Barbe was again seen on the streets, he made no move to renew his trouble with Dix Ryder. On the contrary, when he spied Dix approaching, Barbe always crossed to the opposite side of the street. Once Ryder encountered Hugo Ridge. Politely, Ridge addressed him as "Mister" Ryder, and passed quickly by, not even showing any visible evidence that he had noticed Ryder's satiric smile.

During his wanderings about Arboledo, Dix Ryder was continually meeting men he was supposed to know. That entailed more talk than he relished. Somehow, he managed to keep up his presence; at times — and this puzzled him — names seemed to leap unbidden to his lips, names of men he couldn't even remember being coached on. He had, to be exact, fallen into the role of Dix Ryder, with all the versatility of a closely-fitting glove.

Dix had met other ranch owners in the vicinity: Jim Starr, owner of the Star-Cross Ranch; Chuck Albert, of the Rocking-A; and Burt Yocum of the Bench-Y spread. Through conversation with them he had learned, as he'd suspected, that the DR Ranch was the heaviest loser of stock. These other stockmen shrugged off their losses. They maintained they always expected a certain loss by cow thieves,

Indians, or disease, but such incidents didn't seem anything to worry about. They all seemed to feel that Ryder was exaggerating his troubles, and he saw he could expect no help from them. All this convinced him that Wickmann was concentrating his deviltry on the DR in an attempt to wreck the outfit, and thus gain control of the holdings, by the time the T.N. & A.S. Railroad was ready to purchase a right-of-way through the lands.

All this didn't bother Dix too much. Sabina now appeared to feel that Dix had things in hand, but of that Dix Ryder wasn't certain. He could see nothing but trouble before him, until such time as the Wickmann crowd was entirely cleaned out.

His relations with Sabina worried him more. That was what bothered him most. He was seeing Sabina morning and night, across breakfast and supper tables and during the evenings. Her breath had been soft on his cheek as they bent together over the ranch and tally book accounts, which Hugo Ridge had left in a mess, or had ignored altogether. That Dix was in love with Sabina — deeply in love — there was no doubt in his mind. But would she ever become convinced that the real Dix Ryder was actually dead? Somehow, the new Dix

Ryder didn't believe so. The case seemed hopeless, even though Austin — alias Ryder — knew Sabina cared for him. That, she had shown him in so many ways.

Well, he told himself, resignedly, he could only wait and hope. The first thing to do would be to clean up the current difficulties. Once that was accomplished, he'd feel free to press his suit.

Sabina herself was uncertain. They'd seen so much of each other. A certain loyalty was due the real Dix Ryder. Ah, if she could be sure; what was the right step to take? By this time she realized she cared greatly for this strange man who had come into her life. There were periods when a wave of shame swept over her as she pondered whether or not she was being unfaithful to the Dix Ryder she'd married. At such time she defended her actions and feelings on the ground that Santone Austin was so much like the dead Dix Ryder that she wasn't, after all, being untrue to the memory of the man who had died. But had he actually died? That was a thing she found it difficult to believe. Perhaps — she tried to convince herself — Austin was a reincarnation of Dix Ryder. Sleepless, uneasy nights followed such thoughts. That reincarnation business, she told herself sternly, was not at all logical in the clear light of reason — but when were lovers ever capable of clear reasoning?

There came an evening when Dusty Rhodes didn't appear at Flapjack Hannan's supper table. Dix had been riding all day, with Pete Gratton and Amber Odell, gathering in scattered cows from draws and hillsides. Jeff Clayton was in Arboledo meeting each train that stopped. Dix had just washed up and was looking forward to supper, seated across from Sabina, when Pete Gratton came up to the house, looking worried.

Dix rose from the table. "What's up, Pete?"

"Dusty hasn't rid in yet. Did you send him on some special job?"

Dix frowned. "Not special exactly. I told him this morning, when we left, to sort of scour along our south holdings and see if he could pick up any DR critters. He should be back." Dix looked concerned. "I'd hate to have anything happen to the kid. If that blasted Wickmann has been up to any skulduggery —" He broke off. "Might be a good idea if a couple of us rode over that way."

"That's what I was thinkin'," Gratton nodded.

"Dix —" Sabina began. She looked worried.

"Won't take us long, Sabina," Dix interposed. "Now don't you fret. Keep this supper warm. I'll be back shortly."

At the mess table, Flapjack was just easing into a bench for his own supper. Amber Odell was through eating, and wanted to go in the search for Dusty.

Dix, Amber, and Gratton saddled up and headed off toward the south. There was still a faint light in the west. It wasn't completely dark as yet, though a few stars were twinkling in the eastern sky. A soft breeze brought the fragrance of sagebrush to the riders' nostrils, but they scarcely noticed that as they pushed toward the south, faces grim and set.

Gradually, it became darker as the horses pounded on, with no sign of the missing Dusty Rhodes.

"By God," Dix swore once, "if anything has happened to that kid, I'm going into town and burn a forty-four slug through Purdy Wickmann — or choke hell out of him until he's ready to talk!"

"You figure Wickmann's behind this?" Gratton's voice carried across the intervening space between riders.

"Behind what, exactly?" Odell asked

158

from the other side of Dix.

Dix uttered a short self-conscious laugh. "That's right, Amber, check us up. We don't know that anything has happened to Dusty — yet. It's just damn' unusual, that's all. Trouble is, I'm ready to suspect the worst, and where said worst is concerned, I figure Wickmann must be back of it."

The men fell silent and the horses loped on, their faces stern in the dim light from stars.

Abruptly, Gratton called, "Hold it. I hear somebody comin'."

The horses slowed pace. Dix said, "I was just about to mention I heard somebody. Thought I heard cows bawlin'."

"Me, too," Odell agreed.

Five minutes later they could make out the outlines of a small bunch of cows, with a rider near them, who was uttering sounds of profanity as he urged the reluctant animals along.

Dix raised his voice: "Hallo, the herd!"

There came an instant response. "That you, Dix?" sounded through the darkness. It was Dusty Rhodes' voice.

A feeling of relief swept through Dix and the others. "And Pete and Amber," he called back. "What in the devil's kept you?"

The horses closed in rapidly now.

"This bunch of blasted, reluctant, stub-born, fly-bit cows," Dusty replied. "Cripes! Am I glad to see you hombres!"

The cows slowed down. Dix and the others circled close to Dusty, reining in their mounts on either side of the young puncher. Dix said, "Look like you got quite a gathering, son. Maybe I had a good hunch sending you to our south line —" He broke off, "How many head?"

"Fifty-eight to be exact," Rhodes replied. "And there's something damn' funny about this too —"

"Funny?" Dix asked. "Tell it, Dusty."

The men rolled and lighted Durham cig-arettes while Rhodes explained: "I rode the south stretches like you ordered this morn-ing, Dix, when I left. Didn't see a blasted cow animal. I was about to give up and come back, thinkin' to lend you others a hand. I'd pulled my pony to the side of a tall mesquite to rest him a mite, when I see a cloud of dust comin' up from the south. Another ten minutes and I see this herd headin' this way, with three drivers pushin' 'em on —"

"You mean they were turnin' these crit-ters onto our holdin's?" Dix sounded puz-zled. "Whose riders were they?"

"Dam'd if I know, but s'help me, that's what they were doin'. So I rode out from the mesquite, thinkin' mebbe somebody had herded his cows this way by mistake. I let out a hail, and what do you think happened?"

"I'm waitin' to hear," Dix said patiently.

"There I was," Dusty continued indignantly, "figuring to be friendly. Next thing I knew something like a mad hornet buzzed past my ear and then I heard the report of a .30-30 Winchester. Then the other two riders cut loose with rifles. I caught one slug in the leg. The other bastard missed — what? No, it ain't serious. Already stopped bleedin'. I bandaged it and — t'hell with it, now. Lemme talk. Seein' them galoots was hostile, I slips down from my saddle and shakes a few loads from my forty-five —"

"You slips down from that saddle now," Dix said sternly, "and let's have a look at that wound. You can talk while we examine. Move, cowboy —"

"But, Dix —" Rhodes started to protest.

"*Pronto*, Dusty!" Dix ordered. "Right now."

Grumbling, the young cowhand stepped down from the saddle, and loosened his belt. Matches were lighted. Gratton found

161

a dead mesquite branch which he used to make a small torch.

Dix examined the wound in Dusty's right thigh. The bullet had just furrowed across the skin and while the wound wasn't serious, it had bled profusely as was attested by the blood-soaked bandage Dusty had bound about it.

"Glad it's no worse," Dix grunted. "Wish I had some turpentine —"

"Good you haven't," Dusty stated. "Turpentine stings — ouch!" — as Dix removed a bit of bandanna stuck to the wound.

"I can spit some eatin'-terbacco juice on that scratch," Amber Odell offered.

Dix shook his head. "Amber, hand me my canteen from the saddle."

The wound was washed with water and then Dix rebound it with his own bandanna. Dusty said thanks and climbed back into his saddle.

"Anyway," he continued, as though there'd been no interruption, "my ca'ridges I unloaded was wasted — the distance was too far for good shootin'. While I'm shovin' fresh loads into my cylinder, figurin' I was due for a last ditch fight, them three hombres wheeled their ponies and took off like bats outten hell —"

"Who were they?" Gratton snapped.

"Ain't got no idea. Too far off to recognize 'em, even had I knowed 'em."

"And you mean they run from you?" Odell demanded.

"That's what I'm sayin'. Don't ask me why. I was outnumbered," Rhodes said in puzzled tones. "Could be they thought I had more riders with me, keepin' out of sight behind rocks and trees —"

Gratton extinguished the mesquite torch. Dix asked, "Whose cows are they? Any brands to —"

"Hell, they're our cows — branded plain with the DR iron. Soon as those scuts disappeared, I looked 'em over. They're damn' stubborn to drive — act like they'd been choused too much recently —"

"You're sure they're DR steers?" Dix frowned.

"Well, there's the brands. I even recognized one animal — a line-back with a broken horn that I ain't seen for a few days — 'course it might have been keepin' out of my way. And there's one with a Hereford spot across its eyes, like a bandit's mask. I don't figure there's any doubt. Three or four of 'em looks like they'd been getting ready for brandin' — rope burns on laigs, and a couple shows where the hair had been singed. It's like the thieves had orders to quit right in the middle of the job, and return them cows to us."

Dix gave a short laugh. "Could be that is just what happened. I talked turkey to Wickmann about missing stock. Could be he's stolen these cows, figuring to rebrand 'em and sell 'em below the Border. Then, sudden, he lost his nerve and turned 'em back to our holdin's."

Dusty grumbled. "He lined out a fine job for me, anyway, if that's so. I've had the hell and all, keepin' those brutes moving. They'd mill around and want to settle for the night. Then one would take off on his own with me after him. By the time I'd herded him back, I'd find the rest bedded down and all bawling for water. Then I'd get 'em on their feet and travelin', again. We hit a water hole and I got busy and fixed my laig, sort of, then I had the trouble of gettin' the damn critters started again. All the time I was wishin' I had some help and more ropes. Then — then — you fellers arrived."

"You've done a good job, Dusty," Dix complimented. "Well, let's get these beasts moving again."

It was midnight by the time Dix re-entered the house. A single lamp burned low in the front room, where Sabina sat by a fireplace of slow glowing embers. A look of gladness came into her face when Dix crossed the floor and she got to her feet.

"Oh, Dix, I'm so glad you're back. I was worried — so worried."

He could see her eyes were moist, and it shook him a little. "Nothing to be worried about," he stated, and seating himself near her explained what had taken place.

When he had concluded, she asked, "And Dusty was wounded?"

"I wish you'd take a look at his leg, Sabina. I fixed it as well as possible, but Porky said you'd had some medical training and —"

"Did he tell you I'd never finished my training? Wait, I'll get some bandages and things from the emergency chest, and I'll go back to the bunkhouse with you."

At the bunkhouse, Sabina deftly washed, medicated and rebound the wound with fresh bandages. Rising from her task, she said, "There, you'll be right as rain in a few days. It's not serious, Dusty."

Dusty said thanks and commented, "I'd be right as rain now, if somebody will get Flapjack to stir his hoofs and bring me some coffee and grub."

While the others laughed, Sabina and Dix returned to the house. In the front room, Sabina said, "I'll bet you're hungry, too, Dix. I've kept supper warm in the oven, and I'll have it on the table in a jiffy."

Dix said, "Sabina — wait a moment."

She turned to face him, eyes wide. Even then, before he, himself, realized it, she knew what was in his mind. All her instincts were in revolt. Something told her to go to her room and shut the door. Something else contradicted that feeling. She stood facing him, a loose wrapper of some blue material gathered about her.

"What is it, Dix?" she asked quietly, though a tremor shook her voice.

"Sabina, when I first came in, you had been crying. Why?"

"I — I told you I'd been worried all evening, ever since you left I — I —"

"Why were you worried?"

"Of what might happen. It was unusual for Dusty to be so late. And — and then when you left — you and the others — oh, Dix, suppose there'd been an ambush, some sort of trick, and you'd been shot —"

"Do I mean that much to you, Sabina?" and his voice wasn't quite steady.

"Dix — you — you mean so much —" She broke off.

And then, before either quite realized

how it happened, she was in his arms and he was holding her close, feeling the soft warm flesh beneath her clothing, and her lips were seeking his in a long embrace.

A few moments only and then he felt her arms leave his neck and her hands were pushing against his chest. "Dix, we — you — I — Dix, we mustn't."

"I want to know why," he said tenderly. "Sabina, you're all I've ever wanted —"

He tried to draw her close again, but she resisted. "Oh, Dix — don't. Please understand. Put yourself in my husband's place. Suppose you were to return and learned I'd — I'd been unfaithful to another man, had given way to a momentary weakness? Would you want the woman you loved to be unfaithful while you were absent?"

Ryder pondered the question, heart beating with love, desire, while the girl stood back, facing him, her cornflower eyes brimming with a tenderness she couldn't control.

He stood, frowning, shaking his head almost dumbly, trying to understand. "But — but, how long, Sabina, must we wait?"

"I don't know, Dix. We'll — we'll just have to be patient, and let me go on depending on you, as I've become so accustomed to doing. Oh, Dix, dear, can't you see this isn't for us — now?"

Slowly, he nodded, gaining a stronger control over his emotions. "Yes, I understand things from your standpoint — but not from mine, and I never will. I am as I am. I don't change readily." With an effort he forced a smile. "All right, Sabina, you're the boss. But you know, a good boss feeds her hands well. Didn't you say something about a supper being kept warm in the oven?"

Chapter XIII

The sky was just beginning to gray the following morning, when there came a sudden rush of pounding hoofs toward the house. Then the thundering report of a Colt's .45, followed by more violent explosions. Men were yelling and loosing their six-shooters in the air in an over-exuberance of feeling. Their horses drove past the house and down toward the bunkhouse, where lights had begun to spring into being.

Dix Ryder's head jerked up from the pillow, then he leaped out of bed and raised his window shade. There was nothing to be seen by this time, except the slow-lighting range, but once, through the noise, he caught Jeff Clayton's voice. A slow grin crossed his face, as he donned his sombrero and then began to struggle into his trousers. A moment later he was leaving his room.

He heard Sabina's voice and looking back saw her blue eyes wide with wonderment, peering around the door of her room. "Dix! Good grief! What is going on?"

He laughed. "It's all right, Sabina. Go back to bed."

"Those men you were expecting?"

"I reckon so. They're a hard gang to hold down."

She looked relieved. "All right, I'll go back and finish my beauty sleep," she laughed.

"That," he replied, "is something I never thought you needed."

Her soft laugh followed him as he left the kitchen door and started to cross the patio. Jeff Clayton was just coming in by the back entrance. "Just coming up to get you," Jeff started. "There's a wild bunch if I ever —"

Dix grinned. "My hands always were full of pep and vinegar. Hope they don't wear you down, Jeff."

Clayton shook his head. "Not exactly, but I'd hate to face that bunch if they were ever on the loose *against* me."

"Sounds like my boys," Ryder chuckled. "Always rarin' to go."

"You said it," Clayton exclaimed fervently. "They came pilin' outten the caboose of that freight that comes through, carryin' saddles and war-bags. They was ready to bust down the doors of the livery to get hawsses when I couldn't wake up the proprietor fast enough. Then they wanted drinks, of course. All the saloons was shut up by this time. I finally persuaded them to leave without bustin' in any doors. Dam'd if I know where they're gettin' all their energy. They ain't slept much, jumpin' from train to train to get here fast's possible. And I don't figger they've et much, neither. I roused out Flapjack and told him to get a big bait on the table *pronto*. Them hombres are sure anxious to see you —"

"You warned 'em I was to be called Dix Ryder?" Ryder asked sharply.

Clayton nodded. "Once out of Arboledo, I pulled 'em all to a halt and explained matters. For the first time they quieted down while I talked. All of them seemed to understand. When we got here I made 'em acquainted with Pete and Amber and Dusty — say, what's this about Dusty gettin' wounded and some cows turned back to us?"

"You'll get the details later. Come on, I want to see the boys."

Loud talk greeted them as they approached the bunkhouse. As Dix and Clayton entered the building, a loud cry went up and there were cheers for Dix Ryder. So, they were remembering, Ryder thought. Then came a single voice, "Santone — !"

Two other punchers quickly seized the offending speaker and slammed him under the long table. Dix laughed, saying easily, "I see Hub Wheeler is always ready to boast about his home town — San Antonio." So that mistake was covered all right, as a very red-faced man named Wheeler crawled to an upright position from beneath the table. The men, most between their twenties and thirties, crowded about Dix, shaking hands and pounding him on the back, while Dusty, Pete Gratton, and Amber gazed in some amazement at the vociferous greetings extended their boss.

Gradually, things quieted down. Ryder mentioned names to the regular DR hands. All wore puncher togs and carried holstered Colt guns at their thighs. Sombreros were shoved to the backs of heads; bandannas knotted about the necks. Their overalls and denim shirts looked well-worn — as did their gun holsters.

There was Waco Welch, stolid and muscular, with dark hair and the map of Ireland on his face. Slivers Wood, tall and gangling, with drawly speech. Hub Wheeler, built like a beer keg with tousled hair. Pinto Sanford, red-headed and freckled. Mateo Ortega, slim and definitely Mexican, lithe as a cat. Neil Holland with fighting jaw, inclined to temper. Matt Kimball, Ryder's former foreman. He was the oldest of the bunch, and there were gray flecks in his brown hair, and he had a lined bronzed face.

"And," a voice said as Ryder completed the introductions, "you'll not be neglecting an old friend, I hope er — Dix."

The speaker had been lounging, drowsily, on a chair in one corner of the room. Now he stood erect to reveal himself. Here was the exception in clothing — and other things. He was a short, fat-bellied man with apple cheeks and bald head — so much of the head as could be seen beneath a rusty-black derby hat. With a once-white shirt, he wore a celluloid collar, likewise stained, and a black bow-tie. The bottom of what had been a frock coat was sheared off to fit the rotund body and the skinny legs beneath, wearing Oregon breeches, gave the man all the appearance of a tadpole. His shoes — perhaps it is better the shoes be overlooked.

"Charlie — Charlie Tann!" Ryder exclaimed. "Why, you old gaycat, I didn't expect to see you. Didn't you understand things might get rough here?"

Charlie Tann yawned widely. "Just came along for the show — a spot of entertainment, you might say." He came across and shook Ryder's hand warmly. "It is good to see you again, — er — Dix."

"But there'll be riding maybe, hard riding," Dix protested. "You couldn't sit a saddle unless you were roped in the seat."

"True, true," Charlie Tann conceded in a bored murmur, "but you'll admit, Dix, that I got here as soon as the rest. With full expediency, you might say."

A snicker broke from Matt Kimball. "Yeah, he got here — sittin' back of my saddle. Complained of gettin' saddle sores, too, on the way."

"Such a means of locomotion is sheer torture to one of my upbringing," Charlie Tann protested. "Not to bring into the conversation regarding the odoriferous taint of horse which I find indelicate —"

Yells and hoots cut him short. Ryder caught his shoulder and shoved him back where he could get a good look. "If I remember correct," Ryder stated, "I bought you a complete new outfit of togs before I left Texas, Charlie —"

"Quite true, quite true," Tann nodded,

"but you must understand it is such a chore becoming accustomed to raiment before it is properly suited to one's frame —"

"And," Ryder grinned, "once a hobo, always a hobo."

Charlie Tann looked pained. "I prefer to be termed a Knight of the Road."

"Have it your way, Sir Tann," Ryder laughed. "But what did become of the togs?"

"They were lost, due to a combination of unfortunate circumstances," Tann explained gravely. "There were these two little cubes of ivory, with black spots on them. I had an implicit faith in my opponent's integrity — until, alas! it was too late. My confidence had been misplaced. After he had departed — wearing my best raiment, as it were — I learned that this vandal had a reputation for always carrying his ivory cubes with irregular markings and slightly weighted —"

"Loaded dice, b'Jasus!" Waco Welch let out a whoop. "You'd never before been a-tellin' us of that, Charlie."

Charlie eyed the speaker with a certain dignity. "One keeps one's griefs, to oneself," he spoke. "Had I admitted I had been seduced by Lady Luck, nay, wronged,

I should only have become an object of ridicule."

There was more laughter. Ryder finally broke in, "Well, we've all got to pitch in and work on the DR, Charlie Tann. Right now, you'd best look up Flapjack and give him a hand with the food. I hereby promote you to the job of chief potato-peeler and assistant dish-washer — at the usual wages. So shake a hoof, Charlie. With this gang, Flapjack is going to need a helper."

Charlie Tann bowed his head in humble subjection. "As I travel through this vale of tears," he murmured, "I find that some one is always finding tasks for me."

He departed slowly in search of Flapjack Hannan, followed by some laughter.

Matt Kimball asked, "When do we start getting busy around here, Dix? Jeff Clayton said there were some coyotes on this range giving you a tough time."

"You boys have had a tough time getting here so fast, and I appreciate it," Ryder said slowly. "And it's damn good to have you all here —"

"I'd brought more hands," Kimball said, "except all your old crew weren't still around town — some had found other jobs, some had gone home to visit parents. And knowing you wanted help fast, I didn't want to waste time."

"You've done plumb elegant, Matt," Dix responded. "But don't be in too much of a rush. Jeff's my rod, at present, and we'll figure out the best thing to do later. Meanwhile, after you've finished with the bait Flapjack is fixing, you all turn in and get some shut-eye. Later in the day you can pick out your horses and ride into Arboledo to return those livery crow-baits you rode out on. It'll give you a chance to look over the town and get acquainted sort of."

They talked a few minutes longer and then Ryder left the bunkhouse followed by Jeff Clayton. Outside, the two men paused a moment and rolled cigarettes. Gray smoke mingled with blue and spiraled toward the fast-graying sky overhead. A faint morning breeze lifted above the range.

Jeff said, "It's a good looking crew, Dix."

"None better."

"I'm beginning to feel it's good to have 'em here, helpin' us."

"They'll do all of that, if the going gets too tough. I'd back every man to the last ditch."

"I was thinking, Dix, so long as Matt Kimball used to be your foreman —"

"Hold it, Jeff. I know what you're thinking. Forget it. I named you to rod the DR and that's your job. Matt will understand and help you all possible. He's got more cow knowledge than any hombre I ever knew. So you're still the DR foreman, and the rest will take your orders. There'll be no trouble that way."

"Thanks." Clayton frowned. "There's just one thing I can't quite savvy. Where's this Charlie Tann feller come in?"

"Charlie?" Dix laughed, took a final drag on his cigarette and killed the butt under his booted foot. "Charlie will help in his own way, I figure. He's been with me for a long time, now. Naw, he's no cowman. But he's a good man to have around a bunkhouse, keeps a crew cheered up with his antics. And he'll prove a help to Flapjack, you'll see —"

"But he seems to be just a bum, a tramp, in spite of the talk he spills."

"He is — or was. Secretly, I've always considered him my luck piece. Luck seems to come my way when he's around. I always like to have him at my shoulder in a card game. Why, once I won a pot that'd make your eyes bulge —" He broke off. "But that's another story. And there was a time when I figure he saved my life —"

Again, Dix paused, a frown creasing his forehead, then finished, "But that's another story too. I sort of forget details right now, but someday I'll tell you."

Clayton nodded. "Mebbe there's more to Tann than appears on the surface."

"That's about it," Dix nodded. "Years ago, he used to be a school teacher, and then, as he expressed it one day, he just got tired out with trying to knock knowledge into knuckle-heads. So he quit and took to the road, seeing the country as he expressed it, eating and sleeping where and when he could, with no responsibilities to bother him. That manner of his, I figure, is just put on, it's a sort of pose he takes because he knows it amuses folks. At heart, he's a clown, more than a hobo — but there's more to him than that."

"I'm beginning to understand."

"You'll like him better when you get acquainted. I've got to get back to the house. Sabina was up when I left — like's not in the kitchen, cooking breakfast. She'll be waiting to hear about our — her — new crew."

Clayton said good night, or good morning, and they parted.

Chapter XIV

Ryder slept later than usual the following morning. When he and Sabina had completed breakfast he went to the bunkhouse. Most of the newcomers were still stretched in bunks with a variety of snores assailing the air. Clayton, Odell, Gratton, and Dusty Rhodes were awake and dressed.

"Cripes!" Ryder said, "you hombres should have slept late too — most of your night's sleep was lost." He glanced around. "What became of Charlie Tann?"

Clayton said, "He was dressed when I first woke up. Said he was going down to the cookhouse to lend Flapjack a hand. Cookie hasn't appeared with any chow yet. Reckon the old man is a mite played out."

"Could be, and I couldn't blame him," Ryder nodded. "Dusty, you slip on up to the house. That's Sabina's orders. She wants to look at that bullet slash on your leg and rebandage it."

"Hell," Dusty protested. "Just tell Missis Ryder my leg's all right. No need for her to be fussin' with it. I can ride okay —"

"Slope, Dusty, and fast," Ryder told the youngster. "Didn't you hear me say that was Sabina's orders? 'Sides, Lucia will be there by this time. Don't you want to say 'good morning' to Lucia?"

Dusty Rhodes' face crimsoned. "Aw — aw —" he sputtered, then grinned. "Reckon I'd best obey Missis Ryder's orders." He rose and limped out of the bunkhouse.

The rest laughed when Dusty had gone. Clayton said, "That kid's sure got a sweetenin' on Lucia. Even took her to a dance in town about a month back. Sweet-talks her every chance he gets."

"What's Lucia's attitude?" Dix asked.

"From what I've seen," Clayton chuckled, "the feelin' is sort of mutual. Lucia even baked him a mincemeat pie, one time, supposed to be just for Dusty. Dusty wa'n't here and she left it. By the time Dusty got here there was nothing left but the crust around the rim of the pan."

"Dirty trick," Dix laughed. "Jeff, you and Amber and Pete might ride down along the southern line today. If them Wickmann skunks should show up, be on hand to give 'em a warm greeting should they trespass on our holdin's — unless they

181

bring back more of our cows."

The men departed after they'd had some breakfast. Dusty returned from the house and was ready to take the saddle too, but Ryder vetoed that. "You're not saddling up today," Dix told him. "I don't want you taking chances of catching an infection in that leg." Dusty protested but Ryder was adamant.

"Dammit!" Dix pretended to be irritated. "Nobody's accusing you of shirking, Dusty. You've a job to do here."

"What job?"

"Get acquainted with the new hands. Later, Sabina will come down. She'll need somebody to introduce her, won't she?"

"Ain't you goin' to be here?" the youngster asked.

Dix shook his head. "I've got to ride to Arboledo. You can rep for me while I'm gone. Someday you'll want to be a foreman, and you might as well get some experience now. When the rest wake up and had their grub, tell 'em I left word they were to bring those livery nags to town and return 'em. You can help 'em pick what horses they need from our cavvy — you'll know what's good horse flesh. Give 'em the best. What? No, Charlie Tann won't need a horse. He'll be staying here, mostly."

"Just as you say, Dix," Dusty answered meekly.

Dix nodded. "And tell the boys when they get to town, they can probably find me at Porky Sullivan's bar."

"Yessir, Dix, I'll do that."

Dix turned and left the bunkhouse. Directly after dinner, during which Sabina was unusually silent, thinking of the previous night's happenings, Dix left, went to the corral and saddled up to take off in the direction of Arboledo.

Two hours later he was jogging his horse easily into town. Tying the animal at the hitch-rack before the Arboledo Saloon, he strode on foot from one end of the town to the other, pausing now and then to greet people he was supposed to know, and many others who thought they knew him, and of whom Dix had no knowledge at all. He stopped at a Men's Wear store and had the proprietor make up a bundle of shirts, clean overalls and bandannas, guessing at Charlie Tann's sizes. It made a large bundle and, once more on the street, Dix decided he didn't want to be bothered with it. Then he spotted a small Mexican boy, of about twelve, lounging against a hitch-rack nearby.

"Hi, son," Dix greeted him. "You want

a job?" he asked.

"*Buenas tardes,* Señor Ryder," the boy replied. "The job —"

"Oh, you know who I am?"

"Av-er-yone knows of the Señor Deex Ryder," the boy replied gravely, shuffling his bare feet, self-consciously, in the dust. "I watch' while you make the fight weeth the hombre name' Barbe. It was the good fight — but you ask me about do I want the job. *Si,* Señor Ryder."

"Have you got a pony?"

The *caballo?* The *cuballo* I do not possess, but —"

"We'll hire one. Come on. I want this bundle delivered to the Señor Charlie Tann at the DR Ranch. Can you find it?"

"*Si, señor.*"

The boy followed him to the livery stable where a horse was procured for the boy. Dix watched him ride off with some amusement, proudly erect in the saddle, the bundle clutched tightly under one arm. "You'd think," Dix chuckled, looking after him, "he was one of the conquistadors of Old Spain." Dix had tucked a bill in the boy's pocket.

"Good kid, young Narcisso," the livery man spoke. "No parents. I dunno how he lives. Small jobs and errands for folks around town."

"That so?" Dix was interested. "Maybe I can find him something to do at the DR." He changed the subject. "A bunch of my boys got horses from you last night. They'll be returning them this afternoon. How much do I owe you?"

The man mentioned the amount due and Dix paid him. The fellow shook his head. "My Gawd, where do you find such hombres? Jeff Clayton was trying to quiet 'em down, but they acted like they was ready to tear down my building when they thought I wasn't fast enough. Me, I'd just got to bed when they arrived. They acted like they was a bunch of wolves and it was their night to howl."

Dix laughed. "Just full of spirits, that's all and rarin' to go. Actually, they're a real gentle bunch." He started to leave.

The livery man gazed after him frowning. "Yeah! Gentle — gentle like a hydraphobied she-cougar in matin' season." He shrugged. "Well, mebbe Arboledo could do with a crew like that 'round here. That gang of Wickmann followers is just 'bout takin' over the town."

Passing a Ladies' Wear shop, Dix entered and purchased two silk, embroidered handkerchiefs. "For Mrs. Ryder, I presume," the girl behind the counter commented. "How is Mrs. Ryder these days?"

"No, I — this is — Mrs. Ryder? She's fine, just fine."

His eye had been caught by a shawl, displayed on a long counter. It was of deep green silk, embroidered with white and red peonies, with lighter green foliage, and long fringe at the edges.

"What sort of doo-dad is that?" he inquired, thinking how it might please Sabina and go well with her mahogany-hued hair.

The saleswoman looked pleased. "That came clear from China. I just couldn't resist it when the salesman showed it to me. Of course, no one in Arboledo would ever buy it, but it does make an attractive display. It's beautiful. But I suppose I'm stuck with it."

"You're wrong, lady," Dix said. "I'm buying it —"

"Oh, good. Mrs. Ryder will just love it."

"Please wrap the handkerchiefs and shawl in separate packages."

While the sale was arranged and the two packages wrapped, Dix's gaze strayed toward the window of the store and saw an undersized character staring intently at him, an ugly expression on the rather pinched features. Dix wondered who the fellow was, and while he was wondering, the man passed on down the street.

With the handkerchiefs tucked in a rear pants' pocket and the bundled shawl under his arm, Dix left the store, looking both ways along Main Street, but the man had disappeared.

Dix scowled. "I wonder who that hombre was, sizin' me up through the glass," he pondered. "For a runt-sized feller he sure looked mean, like — like he had some grudge against me. Could be he's somebody I'm supposed to know. Well, he's no friend, at least. God, such eyes. They was fair spitting poison at me."

The sun was beating down strong now, and within a few minutes Dix had forgotten the episode. He continued on, along the sidewalk, nodding to men now and then, until he reached the Arboledo Saloon where he turned in.

Porky Sullivan greeted him with a wide grin. "Sure good to have an old customer drop in regular. What'll it be, Dix?"

"This is what I call beer weather, Porky — and a cigar."

Porky dived beneath the counter, grumbling about how his ice was melting fast and if the train didn't drop him off a new shipment soon, his stock would be warm enough to take a bath in. A moment later he placed an opened bottle and glass on the bar in front of Dix, then shoved a box of cigars before him.

"This beer is just right," Dix commented, taking a sip from the glass. "Some hombres aren't satisfied unless it's nigh frozen in the bottle." He chose a cigar and lighted it. Porky whisked the box to his back counter. Dix placed his package on the bar.

Blue smoke floated in layers about the room while Porky and Dix made idle conversation. There were three other customers at the farther end of the bar who had nodded to Dix when he entered, and then turned back to their own interests.

The swinging doors at the entrance banged back hard, and the man who had been watching Dix through the store window approached the bar.

Porky Sullivan came to attention and moved down the bar a few feet. "What'll it be, Heffner?" he asked rather coldly.

"Sack o' Bull," Vince Heffner said in surly tones.

Porky placed Bull Durham and cigarette

papers on the bar. Heffner tossed out a couple of coins and ripped the government seal from the sack, then shook tobacco into a paper. His fingers made deft movements as he rolled the smoke one-handed, then lighted a match on one thumbnail and exhaled a cloud of gray smoke.

Dix Ryder had been eyeing the man in the back-bar mirror. Heffner had the features of a fellow who hated the world. There was something vicious in the man's bearing, something of a cornered rat in his manner. At any moment, Dix half expected him to bare his fangs and attack. "Just what sort of being was this?" Dix asked himself, puzzled. Unconsciously, his right hand slipped down to his gun and loosened it in the holster.

Heffner didn't miss the movement. He turned toward Dix. "What's the matter? I make you nervous?"

That was all the warning Dix needed. This undersized hombre was more dangerous than he appeared at first glance. He was on the prod; no doubt about that, a hint of a challenge had carried through the sneering tones.

Dix laughed softly. "Now, exactly why should *you* think you could make me nervous, mister?"

Heffner glared at him. Momentarily he seemed at a loss for an answer. There was something queer about his eyes. They didn't seem to focus directly. They were flat, opaque, obsidian-like. Dix had seen eyes like that in sidewinders, ready to strike — only these eyes seemed twice as venomous.

Heffner shrugged bony shoulders. "That's whatever, hombre. I understand you're the famous Dix Ryder, gun fighter, rough citizen."

By this time Porky and his other customers were listening intently. Porky slowly shook his head at Dix. There was a warning there, but Dix was too closely watching Heffner to see it.

Again Dix laughed. "I make no claim to being a gun fighter, or famous or tough."

"I've heard different," Heffner half snarled, exhaling a puff of cigarette smoke in Ryder's direction.

Dix moved on the offensive now. He grinned. "You'd better tell your nurse to clean out your ears. You aren't hearing straight."

A scowl twisted Heffner's pinched features. That wasn't the reply he had expected. "I'm Vince Heffner," he stated, flatly.

"Really?" Dix mocked him. "Sure, I've heard of you. Used to teach Sunday School in El Paso — or was it Tucson — didn't you? It's sure fine to see a better type people coming to Arboledo. And you're going to start a new church here?"

A couple of snickers were heard at the far end of the bar.

"Gawddam it, no!" Heffner said furiously. "I — I never —" He went off into a fit of cursing, half puzzled by Ryder's attitude. Ryder didn't appear to be taking him seriously. It wasn't at all as Heffner had planned. Start a quarrel and then go for his gun. That was Heffner's way. But Ryder wasn't reacting as victims usually did, and the man didn't quite know how to attack such a problem.

Ryder waited until Heffner's profanity had died down to an angry sputtering. "Look here, youngster," he said soothingly, "something seems to have upset you. Stomach trouble, maybe too many lollipops, today? Maybe we'd best get a doctor and feed you some soothing syrup. I don't like to see any human being in pain —" He broke off, to ask curiously, "You are human, aren't you?"

Heffner just stared at him. He'd never encountered anybody like this and he was momentarily thrown off balance. "Hell," he mumbled uncertainly, "You don't get me. I just come in to get acquainted —"

"That's fine," Ryder beamed. "Sorry I misunderstood. I should have realized right off, you were off your feed and it threw you into a tantrum. Porky, set 'em up for me and my old friend, Heifer — no, sorry, I mean Heffner — but don't give him anything stronger'n sarsaparilla — y'know, he's got a weak tummy."

Color flowed into Heffner's sallow features, but the mention of "sarsaparilla" placated him somewhat. Porky hustled to fill orders and learn what was wanted by the three men at the end of the bar.

"Y'know," Heffner stated, cuddling the sarsaparilla in one fist, "under some circumstances you wouldn't be a bad hombre." He took a long drink from the glass of sweet liquid, while Dix was pouring beer in his glass.

"That so?" Dix asked affably. "For instance, what circumstances?"

"Might be we'd be friends, Ryder — like if you ever had trouble with anybody, my gun's at your service."

"You mean if the price was right?" Dix asked carelessly.

Heffner stared at him a moment, glanced

around the room, then gave an almost imperceptible nod.

"Well, thanks, Vince. Dam'd if you haven't got a heart the size of a mustard seed. Lemme see, now —" while Heffner was wondering, puzzled, what a mustard seed looked like. "You mean that thing in your gun holster really shoots —" Again, Dix broke off. "My God, what's that thing in your holster?"

Startled, Heffner glanced down, peering pridefully at the notches cut in the butt of the Colt gun. "That — that's just my iron. What's wrong — ?"

Dix expelled a very loud sigh of relief. "My mistake. For a minute there I thought you'd started taking in washing."

"Washing?" Heffner repeated dumbly.

Dix nodded. "You've cut so many slashes across that butt, it looks like a washboard, Heffner."

Abruptly, Heffner's face became contorted with rage. For the first time he realized that Ryder had been joshing him. "Goddam you," he jerked out, scarcely able to formulate words. "You — you think you're funny, don't you?" Enraged, he dashed his glass on the floor where it shattered to bits. Even in his extreme anger, he realized this was no time to draw his gun.

His whole body was shaking like an aspen leaf in the wind.

Suddenly, Ryder's manner changed. His eyes narrowed to thin slits. His voice came like a blast from the polar regions. "No, Heffner, I don't think I'm funny, but *you* are! Not only that you're too stupid to realize it. Now, get out of here. If you're smart at all, you'll get out of Arboledo. It will be the worse for you if you don't. Now, go on get moving — damn fast!"

Momentarily, Heffner's courage had fled. Once he made a move toward his gun and then stopped, when a loud laugh from Dix further shook his nerve. Half stumbling, he turned and made his way through the swinging doors to the street.

There was laughter from the customers at the far end of Porky's bar, as the three men hurried to finish their drinks and get out on the street where they could relay the news. One man stopped as he was passing. "Nice work, Dix," he complimented. "Arboledo has finally got somebody with the nerve to talk back to Heffner. He's too ready to fight as a rule, been pushin' fellers around all over town. You handled that just right. Now, we'll see if he has the nerve to stay here."

Dix's face sobered when the men had

left. He said to Porky, "I'm not sure I have stopped Heffner. That cuss is vicious, and I figure he's fast with a gun, as well. That look in his eyes is enough to chill a man's spine."

"Never saw such eyes," Porky nodded. "Reminds me of a gila monster I cornered one time. You'll be wise to keep an eye open for Heffner, though — if he stays here."

"He'll stay," Ryder nodded thoughtfully. "I shook him up a mite for the time, but once he has a chance to cool down — hell's bells! he'll have to stay. From now on I figure he'll be ready for the first chance to get his reputation back. That kind don't quit easily." Dix picked up his package from the bar. "I've got to be getting back. Figured my crew would be riding in by this time —"

He broke off, as Matt Kimball entered, followed by Welch, Wood, Wheeler, Sanford, Ortega, and Holland. "Oh, here they are now," Dix resumed. "Hi, gang! Porky, do something with your bottles for this crew of overworked cow-nurses. Matt, did you return the broncs to the livery?"

"Just left there," Kimball nodded. "On the way in we passed a Mex kid who asked the way to the DR. He had a package —"

"Yeah, he's doing an errand for me."

Spur chains rattled across the floor as the crew bellied up the bar while Porky shoved out drinks. Kimball indicated the package Dix was carrying. "Looks like you've been doing some buying yourself."

"Something I bought for Sabina," Dix returned. "I've got to get shoving along."

"Aren't you going to wait for us?" Kimball asked.

"No. There's your drink, Matt. Better wash the alkali out of your gullet." He spoke to the rest, "You boys take it easy and don't rush back. Stick around a spell and learn the town. It might come handy later. If you have any difficulty, let out a yelp for the marshal — Finch Orcutt. He's a right hombre and a good friend of mine. Jeff Clayton has told you about this Wickmann character. He's got considerable following in Arboledo. I don't figure they're all on his payroll, but they'd like to be, and are ready to do anything to get on his good side. Now, I'd hate to hear of you having any trouble with such scuts, so don't start any fracas."

He paused to let the words sink in, while the men listened intently, swung back from the bar. Then he gave a slow wink, adding, "I sure hate trouble. There's a tough J.P.

here. He's got a weasling habit of fining fellers five bucks for disturbing the peace — and I wouldn't want to have to pay more than five for any of you."

Laughter followed the words. Dix went on, "Wickmann's got a gambling joint here. I understand his games are crooked, so act accordingly. One thing, should any of you happen to encounter a hombre named Heffner, have nothing to do with him. I mean that," he added, looking sternly at the crew.

Ortega asked, "Ees hees name Vince — sort of small, hombre, with the very mean face and a — a — I don't know how to say — a look of glass in his eyes — ?"

"That's it," Dix nodded. "Hard, glassy, mean. You know of him, Mateo?"

"*Si, si,* Deex. Een El Paso and other places. A ver' bad reputation — fast with the gun — a killer. He is here?"

"I saw him this afternoon. Porky will tell you what happened. I've got to slope. Just keep your eyes open, that's all."

Good byes were said and he left the saloon to find his horse at the hitch-rack, then climbed into the saddle, turning his mount toward the trail to the DR.

The sun was lowering toward the peaks of the Sangriento Mountains when Dix first sighted the house. A feeling of gladness swept through him. Home! And Sabina. What more could a man ask? Then a frown creased his forehead. How much longer could he call this place home? He was sailing under false colors, as it were. Sabina was certain the real Dix would return, some day. But who was the real Dix? He had fallen so easily into the role he played, that he almost believed . . . He shook off the mood, straightened in the saddle. By God, he *was* the real Dix Ryder.

For the present, anyway. There seemed nothing to do but pursue the course he had chosen. Dix touched spurs to his horse and swept around the house to the corral. Dismounting, he lifted his saddle to the top bar of the corral, and headed for the bunkhouse. Here he found Charlie Tann, Dusty Rhodes, and the small Mexican kid, Narcisso. Charlie Tann had already donned his new clothing. He rose and swept Ryder a deep bow.

"You insist on me being clothed as a gentleman," he said to Dix. "My thanks. For the present I'll attempt to maintain the pretense." The derby hat was tilted to one side of his head.

Dix laughed. "First time you hit

Arboledo, get yourself a new Stet hat, Charlie. And those shoes —" He paused, eyeing Tann's disreputable footwear.

"Just nicely broken in," Tann said lightly. "Perfectly adapted to my pedal extremities, as it were."

"Cripes, Dix," Dusty was saying, getting to his feet, "I didn't hear you ride in. I'll go take care of your hawss —"

"I'm still able to unsaddle and turn him into a corral, Dusty," Dix smiled.

Narcisso was also on his feet. "Eet is time I make the return," he was saying. "The Señor Hannan has fed me well, and I —"

"My Gawd," Dusty exclaimed, "you should see this kid eat — like he hadn't had a bait for a couple of days."

"But one day, *señor*," Narcisso corrected politely. "But only yesterday, I had the sack of peanuts —"

"Where do you sleep, Narcisso?" Dix eyed the boy curiously.

"Een the hay of the liv-er-y stables," Narcisso explained. "And now I go to make the return the *caballo*," — starting for the door.

"I'll see that the horse is returned, Narcisso," Dix said. "You stay here. Maybe Flapjack can find some chores for you to

199

do. We eat regularly around here. Stay on and get acquainted with the rest of my crew when they come in."

"*Gracias,* Señor Ryder." The boy resumed his seat, showing very white teeth in a wide grin.

Dix left the bunkhouse, jerking his head to Dusty Rhodes as he departed. Dusty followed him outside.

"Make out all right, this afternoon, repping for me?" Dix asked.

"No trouble a-tall," Dusty responded. "I took the new hands up to the patio and introduced them to Missis Ryder. She give us all pie and coffee. It all went off easy."

"Fine." Ryder reached to a hip pocket and produced a small package. "Dusty, I figured you deserved something extra for taking care of my job, this afternoon. Happened to see these ladies' silk handkerchiefs and bought 'em. Had an idea you might think of something to do with them."

Dusty beamed. "Lucia —" he started, and then stopped, face flooding crimson. "Sure, sure, Dix. Thanks. I'll take care of 'em."

Dix nodded and continued on his way back to the house. Sabina met him at the door. He started to kiss her in greeting, but she drew back, then proceeded into the front room where a glass and bottle stood awaiting him on a small table. "Something to wash the dust out," she said lightly. "I heard you ride in. Oh, yes, Dix, Dusty brought your new crew up and introduced me this afternoon."

Dix poured a drink after placing his bundle on the table, and relaxed in a chair. "What do you think of the gang?"

"They all looked mighty capable to me," Sabina replied promptly. "None of the bashful shuffling of feet like you'd ordinarily expect. I must say they all had a sort of devil-may-care expression in their eyes, as though — as though trouble never bothered them much."

Dix laughed. "You described 'em. Those are the only sort of hands I'd hire on the Monarch Ranch, back in Texas. We used to run into trouble of one sort or another, at times and —"

Sabina interrupted. "What's in that package you carried in?"

Dix tossed it across to her chair. "Something I saw in a store. It sort of reminded me of you, and I figured you should have it."

Fingers trembling slightly, Sabina

unwrapped the Chinese shawl and shook out its folds. She rose, tossing it about her shoulders, glancing down in pride at the white fringe, incredible oranges and greens and crimsons of the embroidery.

"Heavens, Dix," and her voice wasn't quite steady. "It's — it's beautiful —"

"Plumb appropriate for a beautiful woman," he laughed, enjoying her delight in the shawl.

"This — this — buying this shawl for me," she told him, "is exactly like something Dix used to do."

"I am Dix Ryder," he told her. "Have you forgotten?"

She crossed to his side and for a moment he thought she was about to bend down to him, then she abruptly straightened, saying, "Thank you so much, Dix. And now I must get out to the kitchen and see how Lucia is doing with the supper things. With the enlarged crew to do for, I told Flapjack he needn't bother with the house cooking. Lucia and I can get the supper things up here."

Sometime during the night, Ryder was roused from sleep by the noise of approaching riders. As they drew near the house he caught the sound of laughter and singing. They quieted down as they passed the house and the hoofbeats died out on the way to the corral. Ryder grinned in the darkness, rolled over and went back to sleep.

Chapter XV

The following morning, Dix arose early, dressed and made his way to the mess shanty where the crew was getting breakfast at a long table. Dix stood scrutinizing the group for a moment, then let out a huge whoop of laughter. The men eyed him, grins crossing their faces. Catching sight of Flapjack, Dix said, "I'll catch my bait here this morning," he told the old cook.

The men were too busy stowing away food to do any talking. Narcisso was alertly helping to serve the platters of beans and sowbelly. Large coffee pots were passed along the table. Dix found a seat on the long bench and reached for a slice of sour dough bread. He asked for Charlie Tann and Narcisso informed him that the Señor Tann was helping Flapjack in the kitchen.

Dix chuckled as he gazed at his crew. Of the new men scarcely a one appeared without damage of some sort. There were torn shirts, black eyes, bruises on cheekbones and knuckles. One of Hub Wheeler's ears was swollen to twice its normal size.

The right side of Matt Kimball's jaw looked as though it had been massaged with coarse sandpaper. Scarcely a man was lacking some sort of contusion. Ortega's lower lip was puffed and red, preventing his usual smile, but his eyes smiled for him when he met Dix's gaze.

Dix observed dryly, "Looks to me as though the DR should lay in a supply of horse linament and a mite of court plaster."

No one answered as the men continued chewing, some, no doubt, with a bit of difficulty.

Dix went on, "Enjoy yourselves last night? How'd you like Arboledo?"

"Sure and we had ourselves a time," Waco grinned, exposing a new vacancy in his row of upper teeth. No one else spoke.

"Nice you found everything friendly," Dix observed, straight-faced, "and didn't run into any trouble."

"No trouble for *us*," from Pinto Sanford. "None of us had more'n seven-eight drinks all evenin'."

"Makes me feel good to hear it," Dix said quietly. "I wouldn't want the DR crew getting a rep for being quarrelsome and getting into trouble when they hit town."

No one replied to that. By this time the men were pushing back plates and empty cups and rolling cigarettes. Matt Kimball said suddenly, "There was a mite of trouble, Dix."

"So? What happened."

Kimball glanced around. "The law-man — Marshal Finch — put me under arrest —"

"For what?"

Kimball shoved back his sombrero and scratched his head. "I ain't sure. I was sort of — er — you might say — well, giving a feller a few pointers in the manly art of self-defense, as they call it."

"Manly art of assault and battery, if I know you, Matt," Dix laughed.

"Uh-huh, well, somehow this feller slipped and fell. He didn't get up for a spell. And then the marshal arrested me. When he found out I worked for you, he let me go. I told him you'd fix things up, first time you went to Arboledo."

"Fine. I'll take care of it," Dix chuckled.

The men were rising from the table now, preparing to head for the corral and saddle up. Dix noticed that each man took a careful look at the gun in his holster, before going out.

Jeff Clayton was smiling as though the

whole story of the previous night hadn't been mentioned to Dix. "Any special orders, Dix?"

"You're the rod, Jeff. Just go on as we outlined."

"I figured to split the hands up with Amber, Pete, and Dusty — Dusty says he'll ride today — and let them get acquainted with our holdin's."

"That's fine. I'll see you all tonight."

A short time later Dix heard the riders moving away from the corral. Clayton came back. "I sure feel better now that we have a real crew to back us — a fightin' crew, I'd say. Wait until you hear the whole story about last night."

"I'll get it from Finch Orcutt, Jeff. I've got to get moving if I want to get to town early."

"One thing, Dix, did you put those hombres up to something?"

"Me?" Dix looked astonished. "I don't have to put those boys up to anything. Somehow, they seem to get ideas on their own."

Clayton just nodded, seeming a bit puzzled. Dix finished his breakfast and a short time later was in the saddle, heading for Arboledo, chuckling to himself as he rode, thinking, "I wouldn't be a mite surprised if that crew astonished a few people last night."

It was just after nine o'clock when Dix rode into Arboledo. The sun was high, mincing black shadows along one side of the street and in the spaces between buildings. There weren't many people on the street — a few women doing their early marketing and a scattering of men in citizens' togs. Here and there a proprietor was sweeping the sidewalk in front of his store; there was a lounger, now and then, to be seen sitting on a porch to avoid the heat of the day. Mostly the places at hitch-racks were vacant — only a few wagons and ponies were to be seen.

Ryder left his horse at the tie-pole before Marshal Orcutt's office, a blocky building of white-washed adobe, with a jail and half-a-dozen cells at the rear. The office was small, with a roll-top desk, a couple of chairs and bare wooden floor. On one wall was a packing-house calendar. A shotgun and rifle stood in one corner; in another corner a broom rested.

Orcutt swung around in his chair when Dix entered and sat down. The marshal didn't say anything, just eyed Dix steadily for a few moments until Dix started to laugh.

"Tell me," Orcutt said seriously, "just where did you ever find a new crew like that? Do you breed 'em, yourownself — cross a tornado with a keg of gun powder, or what?"

"Just some fellers I happen to know," Dix said quietly. "I understand you had to arrest one of my men last night. What was — ?"

"One of them?" Orcutt exploded. "My Gawd, Dix! At one time or another I had to arrest every damn' one of 'em."

"Interesting," Dix stated carelessly. "Howcome you didn't keep 'em behind bars?"

"Because I had no more bars to keep them behind. My blasted cells were full — jammed full with as many men as I can get in 'em — and they still are." He added darkly, "There's a freight train stops here this afternoon, and I figure to empty my cells then. Certain scuts are due to leave this town fast — and already a lot has already took off on their own —"

"Wickmann followers?"

"No-goods, down-at-the-heel punchers, hoodlums that have created a hell of a lot of trouble in Arboledo, hoping that Wickmann would take notice of them and put 'em on his payroll."

Dix said mildly, "You sound as though there'd been a couple of fights, last night?"

"A couple?" Exasperation swept across Finch Orcutt's features. "That's all there was here last night. While I was breakin' up a fight at one end of the town, I'd hear yells of 'Fight — Fight!' at the other end. Why dammit, I like to run my laigs off, trying to keep up with things goin' on. It plumb wore me out."

"But what started it?" Dix asked placidly. "Those boys of mine are gentle as kittens —"

"Yeah! Tiger kittens!" Orcutt scoffed. "I will say this — I questioned a heap of folks who had no part in the fracas and one and all said that your men didn't start a fight. It just seemed like your men was new in town and the scuts started out to test 'em — well, they found out all right."

"Much shooting?" Nix asked.

"Now that's a queer thing," Orcutt frowned. "I couldn't find one bit of proof that any of your men had jerked an iron. Some of the hoodlums tried, but never got a chance to use their guns — they hit the floor too fast — and a lot of 'em didn't get up right off."

"I'm certain glad to hear," Dix grinned, "that my men aren't quarrelsome and go around picking fights —"

"I think you're a liar," Orcutt stated bluntly. "From all I can find out those DR hands came to town just primed for trouble, but were smart enough to let the others start first. And then — *whamo!*"

"But what about these arrests?"

"When I was told they were your men I let 'em go when they gave me their word they'd show up in court if necessary. And then I'd no sooner let 'em go than they'd start cleaning up some other bunch. I finally give up, I was so wore down. I saw the Justice of the Peace, first thing this mawnin' and gave him the names of the DR men. Like I expected, they was each fined five dollars for disturbin' of the peace. I got some of the scuts comin' up before him later to pay their fines. They'll get the same fine, no doubt. I already paid the fines for your men —"

"I'll square up with you —"

"Sometimes I think it was worth it. A lot of coyotes, hoodlums, are getting out of Arboledo —"

"Well, I'm glad there was no real bad damage —"

"No bad damage?" Orcutt interrupted, eyes bulging. "You know what them wild-cats of yours done?"

"I'm waiting to hear," Ryder grinned.

"They went down to Wickmann's bar and gambling house. When they discovered a game was run crooked they tipped over the apparatus. That led to more fightin'. Then they headed for the bar. Chairs and other 'quipment is broken, the bar mirror smashed. Wickmann —"

"Now that's a real pity," Ryder said in a mock sympathetic tone. "Tell me more."

"Wickmann was in a spell back, mad as a wet hen. He threatens to sue you for damages."

"I'll be glad to listen to Mister Wickmann's tale of woe anytime he feels like complaining to me. Now I'm real worried."

"In a pig's eye you are," Orcutt said sarcastically. "Tell me, Dix, did you put your hands up to doing all that?"

"Now, you know how fond I am of peace," Ryder said in injured tones. "All I did was just drop a couple of hints that I'd like to see Arboledo cleaned up. Could be the boys got a mite over-enthusiastic."

"Cow-chips!" Orcutt said scornfully. "You and your peace talk — say —" he broke off. "I hear you had some trouble with Vince Heffner, yesterday."

"No trouble for me. I just joshed him a

mite and he lost his temper. What? No, he didn't pull a gun. He was just too mad. All upset like. I expected any minute he'd turn around and bite himself. He was fair steaming when he left."

Orcutt looked seriously at Ryder. "Don't you underestimate him, Dix. He's bad medicine. You'll have to be on the look-out —"

"Was he in any of the scraps last night?"

Orcutt shook his head. "Didn't see him around town all evenin'. Nor Doag Barbe, nor any of the coyotes close to Wickmann. That's queer too. Nigh every night they generally make trouble for somebody. Wickmann wasn't at the gamblin' house when it was wrecked, either. Like's not, him and his scuts is planning some new skulduggery — oh, yes, when Wickmann was in, a while back, he claims he has some sort of proof that you're not Dix Ryder."

"That so?" Ryder's pulse quickened. "What's his proof?"

"He says that Heffner spied on you, yesterday, through the window of Tomkins' Ladies Wear Shop, and saw you buyin' silk handkerchiefs and a shawl — but you had the handkerchiefs and shawl wrapped in separate packages. Wickmann claims that proves you got some woman, 'sides Sabina, on your string. He claims that if you were Sabina's husband, you wouldn't be buyin' doodads for some other woman. So —"

Ryder laughed, extremely relieved, and told Orcutt what he had purchased and why the goods were wrapped separately. "Anyway, Finch, we're getting the town cleaned up to some extent, if the hoodlum type is getting out of Arboledo."

"It helps," Orcutt admitted. "But there's quite a few of the rougher element around yet, who had sense not to get into the fights last night when they saw how things was goin'. As I see it, them that's left is just itchin' to side Wickmann, given an opportunity."

"That sort of thing I've been expecting," Ryder nodded. "I wrote out a paper I'd like to get printed, if that can be done."

"Sure, the local newspaper, the *Arboledo Star* — which is published now and then — handles printin' jobs for folks, posters and announcements and such. They hire help to distribute such stuff too."

Ryder tossed a sheet of paper on Orcutt's desk. Orcutt read it, frowning. "Hmm — Monday night lecture — on crime." He looked up, brow creased. "I don't get it, Dix. Me, lecture? But about what? I can only say we're against crime.

I've said that a hundred times —"

"Listen, Finch, I'll explain." Ryder talked steadily for several minutes. Finally Orcutt's brow cleared and he admitted that Ryder's scheme might work and that it was worth trying, at least.

Dix left the marshal's office and strode off in the direction of the newspaper building. Here he left directions for the printing and posting of his proposed placard. That accomplished, he walked back to his horse, climbed into the saddle and headed for home.

By nightfall yellow placards, printed in heavy black ink had been posted on the fronts of buildings and saloons, placed in bars and tacked to the telegraph poles in the vicinity of the railroad rails. The placards read:

Monday Night
Free Lecture
On
CRIME & LAW ENFORCEMENT!
By
Marshal Finch Orcutt,
Town Hall
8 O'Clock Sharp.

By the time the supper hour had passed,

Marshal Orcutt was being beseiged on all sides by questioners regarding the announcements. When he began to be kidded about being a "silver-tongued orator," he retired in some confusion to the sanctuary of his office, locked the door and sat in darkness, wondering what exactly would emerge from Dix Ryder's plan. Well, it might work.

That night, the town was unusually quiet.

Chapter XVI

Several days passed with no disturbance of any sort, in Arboledo, or out on the range, but it was like the quiet that precedes a terrific storm and the town waited, tense. Dix's new crew, who had already been informed of his plan for Monday night's lecture, meanwhile had labored mightily under Jeff Clayton's directions to gather in the scattered DR cows and bunch them near good grazing and water, where the animals could start to regain lost weight. A study of the tally book showed Ryder that quite a number of head were missing.

Sabina had been curious about the Monday night lecture and wanted to attend, but Ryder vetoed that by telling her it was best she remain at home, in case some trouble did break, which he explained he didn't expect to happen. Nevertheless, Sabina looked somewhat worried when he saddled up and rode off toward Arboledo Monday afternoon. Surely, no just God would allow her to lose Dix a second time.

It was getting along toward supper time when Dix reined in his pony at the hitch-rack of Marshal Orcutt's office. He entered the building and dropped into a chair. "Got your lecture all prepared, Finch?"

"Oh, hullo, Dix. Well, I've figured out a few things to say — sort of stored 'em in my memory. Figured to write 'em on paper, but I couldn't keep an eye on folks, with a paper to read."

"Town keeping quiet?"

"Arboledo is just waitin' — sort of braced — to see what trouble will come of tonight's doin's. Everythin's been quiet — but it's like the quiet of a steamin' kettle before the top blows off."

"Wickmann been in?"

"Several times. He's curious as hell about this lecture, trying to learn what's back of it. Still insists he's goin' to sue you in court for the damage to his gamblin' parlors, done by your crew. He's got a special spite against Mateo Ortega, too. He don't like Mexes, nohow, anyway, and he claims that Ortega knocked his bartender down twice and the man's got a busted jaw —"

"Twice?" Ryder looked surprised. "I'll have to tell Mateo he's slipping. When he was lightweight champion of Mexico City, one punch usually did the job."

"Jeepers! No wonder Ortega can fight."

Dix nodded. "He does a prime job when necessary — with fists, guns, or out range riding — as good a man as I've got on my crew. C'mon, let's find a restaurant. I'll buy you a bait. My stomach is beginning to think my throat is cut."

Shortly before eight o'clock, Ryder and Orcutt entered the town hall, a large false-fronted frame building, lighted by oil lamps spaced in brackets around the walls. At one end of the room was a slightly raised platform on which stood a flat-topped desk and a number of wooden chairs. A town clerk was already seated near the desk. What were known as the town councilmen occupied other seats. All looked a bit uneasy, as though expecting trouble to break at any minute. Faces were extremely grave.

The hall was already filled and there were but few vacant chairs remaining at the rear. Folding seats had been placed in even rows. The clerk had asked several people to bring their own seats, because the number of folding chairs proved insufficient. Ryder and Orcutt made their way to the platform and after nodding to others, took the two vacant chairs that had been held for them.

Ryder ran a quick searching eye over the audience and was glad to note only a scattering of women present. There was no telling what might happen, if worse came to worse. A sudden frown creased his forehead as he saw the first two rows of seats filled with a rather rough-looking element, though with most he'd had no personal contact. Seated in the front row was Purdy Wickmann, but there was no sign of Doag Barbe, Heffner, Alonzo Tidwell and Hugo Ridge. Doubtless, Ryder mused, Wickmann was playing it smart. It was quite likely Wickmann had ordered these men to remain away from the lecture, until he learned what steps Marshal Orcutt planned to take.

Orcutt got to his feet, cleared his throat, and stated, "It's eight o'clock and about time I started. Doorkeeper, will you please shut the door and lock it? From now on, don't let anyone else in, as I don't want any interruptions in our proceedings."

A few in the audience craned their necks in the direction of an elderly doorkeeper, who limped leisurely toward the open door, then lost interest in the proceeding.

They heard the door slammed and a lock

turned after a minute, but no one noticed the quiet entrance of several men who slipped in at the last moment. These men were Ryder's entire DR crew with the exception of Charlie Tann, Flapjack Hannan, and the small Narcisso. These men took up an almost stealthy stance at the rear of the room.

One of the unshaven characters in the front row yelled, "Well, get started, Orcutt. We ain't got all night to waste here." There were some jeering remarks from his companions.

The marshal moved to the desk, again cleared his throat. After a few sentences his self-consciousness disappeared and the words came clearer.

"This lecture," Orcutt stated, "isn't intended to keep you folks here long. I notice a few ladies in the audience, and none of my remarks are aimed at them or at honest business and working men. Mostly, I intend to strike at a certain lawless element which aims to take this town over. And I, for one, don't intend to let that happen — and many others back me up in the thought —"

He paused to catch his breath a second and caustic laughter rose from the front row of seats. A coarse voice exclaimed,

"Quit the windjammin', Orcutt, and come to the point!"

Orcutt's face flushed angrily, "I'll do just that, Randy Buck," he snapped. "I got a list of names here, and yours is on it as an undesirable. The point is, if you're so anxious to have it, that every man on this list appears to have no visible means of support, though a great many of you have money to spend. Where do you get it? Crooked money it looks like to me. Drunken men have been hit on the head and rolled. Too many of you are bullies and start fights. Stores have been robbed. Petty stuff most of it, but it must be stopped —"

A man in front protested, "Some of us win money in Mister Wickmann's place — cards and dice and so on —"

"That," Orcutt snapped, "is a good joke, too. Anyway, Wickmann's gambling house is closed down temporarily — or I'm hoping for good." Wickmann glared angrily and shifted in his seat, but remained silent.

"— so, anyway," Orcutt continued, "Wickmann's place will no longer serve as an alibi. Now I know who works for his money around here and who doesn't. Those who don't have jobs are being asked to leave town — at once!"

"Suppose we don't want to take your orders?" an evil-faced man rasped.

"It's what *we want* — not you," Orcutt exclaimed. "I'm telling you to get out!"

Wickmann was on his feet, face red. "Look here, Orcutt," he blustered, "you can't do this. It's unconstitutional. Just because you got a grudge against certain men, you can't ride roughshod over 'em in this way —"

"That's telling him, Purdy." Several voices yelled encouragement.

Wickmann beamed at the support he was getting. "You see, Orcutt —"

Orcutt's steely tones interrupted, "What's the matter, Wickmann, you worried for fear your name is on my list? I'll tell you, now, it isn't, so shut up until you're concerned."

Wickmann yelled, "We won't stand it —"

One of the rough element whooped, "Go put your haid in a tarbar'l, Orcutt. We ain't none of us goin' to leave until we git ready, are we, boys?"

"NO!" came a thunderous reply.

Wickmann raised one hand to silence them. "Let him talk, fellers, then we'll all go and do some drinking at my expense —

if you don't all laugh yourselves to death at what he says, first." He settled back in his chair again, prepared for considerable amusement at what Orcutt would say next.

When the hall had quieted down again, Orcutt said, "That's just about all I've got to say, folks. So we can get to business."

Silence greeted the words, then Dix Ryder rose. He said easily, "You don't have to turn around, folks, but if you do you'll note that everyone in here is covered. Now, perhaps, Marshal Orcutt can get busy reading his list of names."

Heads turned as though on pivots and then an abrupt silence fell on the audience. Ranged at the rear of the big room, stood every member of the DR crew, drawn six-shooter in hand. A few snickers ran through the room as people realized how Ryder and Orcutt had out-maneuvered the Wickmann faction.

Wickmann leaped to his feet again, face apoplectic. He exclaimed furiously, "It's a put-up job. Don't nobody resist or they'll shoot us down like dogs!"

A woman screamed, several people began talking in fearful tones. A few men dived to the floor. Ryder's voice cut through the beginning bedlam, carrying clearly through the noise.

"Purdy Wickmann lies! No one will be shot unless he starts trouble. I'm asking you all to quiet down while Marshal Orcutt calls off the names on his list."

Quiet again descended. Ryder continued, "As the marshal calls off each name, the name's owner will come up here and deposit his gun, or guns, on the platform next to the desk. And remember, every name on that list is known to the marshal, so I'm advising against resistance. Go ahead, Marshal."

"This is an outrage!" Wickmann bawled furiously. "Don't stand for it, fellas. Keep your guns and —"

His voice died away as no one seemed ready to obey him after a furtive look at the row of grim-faced men with drawn guns at the rear of the hall. Rather the men seemed inclined to slide down in their chairs, as though trying to keep from sight.

Orcutt glanced at his list. "Randy Buck."

All the belligerence had passed from Buck by this time. He rose, shuffled up to the platform and reluctantly placed on the floor a worn-looking six-shooter, then half stumbled back to his seat.

"Joseph Mallory," Orcutt called next.

Mallory, face twisted with fear, rose hastily and surrendered his six-shooter, then meekly tiptoed back to his seat.

"Louis Schlotzer," the marshal read next.

A husky man with a red, unshaven face, half rose and mumbled resentfully, "I ain't agonna give up my gun."

"Suit yourself," Orcutt said carelessly. "I'll just put a checkmark after your name. The men at the back of the hall can take care of you. I might advise against resistance, Schlotzer. I understand the General Store clerk sold quite a number of new hemp ropes today — and I don't mean lariats. Naturally, I'll do all in my power to prevent any illegal" — he stressed *illegal* — "lynchings in Arboledo, as it's against the law, but after all a law officer can't be at both ends of town at once —" This was a matter of bluff on Orcutt's part.

That was as far as he got. The man's resistance collapsed and he quickly came up and placed his gun on the floor.

Name after name was read off from the marshal's list, until fifteen or sixteen six-shooters of various calibers rested on the floor beside the desk, in addition to two Bowie knives. All resistance seemed to have vanished and the hoodlums' spirit sagged.

Wickmann attempted a further protest.

"You can't get away with this, Orcutt," he blazed hotly. "There's other guns to be bought —"

"Exactly, Wickmann," Ryder interposed, "and when we hear of any unusual sale of weapons, we'll know where the money came from. I'd advise you to shut your trap before your name goes on that list. I'm planning to make out a special list for you, and it will be written in *lead*. Is that plain?"

Wickmann had no trouble getting the message. He whirled away and stomped angrily down the aisle between seats to the door. Here the doorkeeper opened up and allowed him to depart.

Finch Orcutt went on. "You fellers who have surrendered your guns can leave the town hall any time you want — but leave Arboledo, as well! Most of you have hawsses. Get 'em and ride — fast! But, get out! Any man of you I see on the street tomorrow mornin', I'll arrest for vagrancy. You've already seen that Wickmann can't help you, so be advised. We're sick of your kind, and we're not putting up with any more scuts such as you —"

But before he could complete the words the hoodlums were scrambling hastily down the aisle toward the doorway, edging somewhat timidly aside as they passed the stern-visaged DR cowhands.

Orcutt and Dix looked after them, smiling. Orcutt raised his voice again, "That's all, folks. Thanks for your kind attention."

The crowd rose from its seats and began to disperse. Several came to the platform to shake hands with Ryder and the marshal. Ryder called to Jeff Clayton at the back of the room,

"That's it, Jeff. You and the rest of the crew can go get a drink, then we'll start for home."

The town hall was darkened by the time Ryder and Orcutt emerged on the street. They stood on the sidewalk talking a few minutes.

"Well, that's another step in the right direction," Orcutt said in some relief. "We'll get rid of a few more coyotes — and my apologies to all coyotes —"

"Skunks would be a better word," Ryder laughed. "And my apologies to skunks, too."

"Think they'll take warnin' and get?" Orcutt said.

"I'm figurin' so. We threw a real scare into 'em, and my hands looked mighty tough back there with their hardware ready. Well, we'll see what move Wickmann will try next. He'll have to act soon. We've whittled down a hell of a lot of his backing and he must be getting nervous. If I can only force his hand into some rash move, we've got him."

Ryder grinned in the darkness. "Before you turn in tonight, Finch, you might sort of spread a rumor that there are a lot of indignant citizens around, talking about tar-and-feathers treatment for any of those galoots that refuse to leave. You can make out that a lot of peaceful citizens have got riled at last, now they see they've got backing. And that they want action — now!"

"Good idea, Dix. If necessary I can turn liar as well as the next man."

The pair walked to the marshal's office where Ryder got his horse, stepped up to the saddle and started for home. A certain thrill always ran through him as he thought of the word *home*. Then a frown drew lines in his forehead. He thought, uncertainly, it was home, wasn't it? Something puzzling there: at times the familiar surroundings seemed as though he'd always known them; at others, he was not so sure of that. He rubbed one hand across his face. How long, he wondered, could he continue to masquerade as Dix Ryder? At present he knew he never wanted to resume his old name; he wanted it to remain Dix Ryder, with Sabina, to the end of his days. . . .

Chapter XVII

A week passed swiftly by, while Ryder waited impatiently for Wickmann's next move. Twice Ryder rode to town to consult with Finch Orcutt. The second time, Orcutt could still throw no light on the subject, and admitted he was puzzled at Wickmann's inactivity. He took a chew of tobacco, masticated meditatively a moment, then sent a thin brown stream to clang against the brass cuspidor, near his desk. Dix, grinning at the unerring aim, shifted in his chair.

"I'm damned if I understand it, Dix," Orcutt frowned. "Each day I brace myself for a trouble that never comes. Maybe we've got Wickmann so worried, he's afraid to start anything."

"Do you believe that?" Dix shot the marshal a skeptical glance.

"No," the marshal grunted, "not none, atall." He spat again.

"Seen any of those scuts we told to clear out of town?"

"You asked me that two days ago when you rode in," the marshal said. "The answer is no different now. Those bastards have gone for good, I figure."

"Not too surprising. They lacked guts, that gang, and only needed to have someone throw a scare into 'em — which we did. When they saw that Wickmann couldn't help 'em out, they saw the writing on the wall and didn't wait to see if Wickmann could come up with some sort of eraser, later."

"I reckon that's about the size of it, Dix."

Ryder looked thoughtful. "It looks to me like Wickmann doesn't have anybody left, except Doag Barbe, Vince Heffner, Hugo Ridge, and Alonzo Tidwell. Seen anything of them?"

"Not of Tidwell and Ridge, no. Barbe and Heffner are still around town, but both seem to have dropped their nasty manners. Damn' quiet — too damn' quiet — both of 'em. Polite as you please, when I pass. Nobody's made any complaints against 'em. Even Wickmann doesn't have much to say when we meet. 'Course, he's rebuilding and fixin' up again down to his gamblin' place, so that could keep him busy —"

"Do you believe that?" Ryder said again.

Orcutt gave a short laugh. " 'Bout as

much as I believe hawsses grow steer horns."

Ryder nodded. "So, Wickmann is just biding his time. Could be he's sent for some hired gun fighters, and is waiting for them to arrive. Or maybe they have arrived. Seen any strangers in Arboledo?"

"Funny you should ask that. I was just about to mention it." The marshal again expectorated. The cuspidor rang like a gong. "Yesterday, five fellers in cow togs rode in — rather rough-lookin' hombres, but nothin' I could really take exception to. They didn't start any trouble, any place, and seemed to mind their own business."

"Said business being?"

"I didn't talk to 'em direct, but they give it out in one of the bars that they were lookin' for jobs, punchin' cows. Like I say, they was peaceful — stopped for a few drinks and a bait and then rode out again —"

"What direction?"

"I was told they headed southwest. They'd been given directions to other ranches hereabouts where they might apply, but I reckon they didn't even try for jobs —"

"Not at the DR, anyway," Ryder said.

"I've talked to hands from the Star-

Cross, Rocking-A, and Bench-Y, when they rode in for mail this mawnin'. They claimed they hadn't seen any five punchers seekin' work at their outfits."

"And they likely wouldn't. You don't often see that many, at once, out looking for work."

"That's true," Orcutt nodded. "So what do you make of it?"

"Any of 'em visit Wickmann's office?"

The marshal shook his head. "Nor did they go near the gamblin' place and bar. I sort of had a weather eye on 'em."

Ryder scratched his chin. "That sort of clears the atmosphere in one direction."

"How do you mean, Dix?"

"First, those five were familiar with the town, or they'd have asked more questions — probably been here before — not all five at once, maybe. So they're not hombres that Wickmann hired recently to settle my hash."

"What makes you so sure?"

Ryder smiled. "Wickmann realizes now that I have a pretty good crew of fightin' men. He'd not be satisfied to just put five new hands on his payroll. He'd know he'd have to have at least twice that to down us, if it came to a showdown. So, I figure those five have been on his payroll right along —"

"That could make sense," Orcutt agreed.

"It's quite likely, Finch, that those hombres are the ones that were stealing DR cows, and that they have some sort of hideout south of our boundary line."

"Possible," Orcutt nodded. "But if they had a hideout southwest of here, they'd have to have supplies to eat on." He frowned. "I've heard of no strangers riding in to buy supplies."

"Wickmann could manage that, a little at a time. And when Hugo Ridge and Tidwell were at the DR, they could have handled things — maybe donated DR grub. A sack of flour one day, a bag of beans another, a slat of sowbelly —" He broke off, "Y'know, Flapjack said one time that our supplies seem to last better than they did. Flapjack's not young any more. It'd been easy to rob things when he wasn't around."

The men talked a few minutes more, then Ryder announced that he'd better be getting back to the ranch. Orcutt asked why he didn't await the cool of the day before riding. Ryder laughed and stated he liked hot weather.

"Just so you avoid hot lead, Dix." Orcutt rose and followed Ryder to the door. "Just be careful who you let get behind you."

"I'll try, Finch, I'll try," Ryder smiled. "*Adiós.*"

He climbed into the saddle and jogged the pony as far as Porky Sullivan's bar. Here he dismounted and after the preliminary greetings, ordered a bottle of beer. Porky set out a frosty-looking bottle and a glass. Ryder took a long drink, set the glass down again.

"That's mighty satisfactual on a day like this," he stated, wiping his lips. "Cool in here, though."

"Not bad, with that rear door open. Lets a draught through. Feller in here a spell back was saying it's the hottest day we've had all year and that folks are staying off the streets."

Ryder nodded. "Now that you mention it, I noticed that Main Street looked sort of empty when I rode here —"

The swinging doors opened and Vince Heffner pushed his way in and up to the bar. Ryder moved half way around from the bar, not knowing what to expect, but Heffner nodded genially enough. "Sack of Durham," he told Porky.

Porky slid the tobacco across the bar and retrieved the coins Heffner had placed there before starting to, one-handed, roll a cigarette.

Ryder said, "Have a drink on me, Heffner — sarsaparilla, I suppose."

"Thanks. Don't care if I do." Something like a smile lighted his face, though his strange eyes appeared as baleful as ever. He stood sipping his drink, while Ryder watched him.

"Look here, Ryder," he said, replacing his glass on the bar, "I figure there's no use you and me bein' on the prod against each other. I'd like to be friends."

Ryder grinned. "No, Heffner, I don't want to hire any gun hands."

"I don't get what you mean, Ryder."

"Didn't you offer to hire your gun to me, last time we met here? To me, Heffner, that sort of looked like a double-cross for Wickmann."

Heffner just shook his head. "No, you mistook me, Ryder, but, y'unnerstand, a man has to make his livin' where the cash is. Actual, Wickmann ain't nothin' to me but a big blow-hard. He's always hinting at ideas I don't like —"

"Such as — ?" Ryder waited.

"Aw, nothin' you'd be interested in. Just say I'm tired of workin' for Wickmann. I figure to blow this town."

"What sort of work do you do for Wickmann?" Ryder asked curiously.

Heffner evaded that. "Well, I got to be shovin' along." He settled his sombrero more firmly on his head. "I'll see you again, Ryder. And thanks for the drink."

"You're welcome," Ryder laughed.

The laugh left his face when Heffner disappeared between the swinging doors. Unconsciously, his hand had crept down to gun butt. Now, he loosened it a couple of times in his holster.

Porky noticed the movement. "That hombre has a queer effect on you, Dix." He gestured toward the holstered gun.

Ryder became conscious of what he had been doing and laughed uneasily. "Yes, I reckon he does, Porky. Somehow, it's like being cornered by a rattler."

He turned back to his beer and drained the glass. Abruptly, he replaced it on the bar and strode toward the doorway, then stepped outside and down to the sidewalk. He found the situation about as he had half expected.

Ryder had sensed, when Heffner left the saloon, that there was some sort of skulduggery in the man's twisted mind. Now, that suspicion was confirmed. There weren't many horses waiting at the hitchrack, and there was a wide space in the road between Ryder's gelding and the next

238

neighboring horse.

Vince Heffner was crouched down at the side of Ryder's horse, a big Barlow knife in his right hand, working the blade in a sort of sawing motion.

Ryder, rounding the end of the hitch-rack, closed in fast. At the sound of his step, Heffner jerked erect, knife still in hand, and then backed away two strides. For a brief moment his opaque, reptilian eyes just stared at Ryder, though the man's features didn't change to any extent. Then his upper lip lifted in a sort of snarl, and he started to lift both hands in the air, as though in surrender.

"So that's your game," Ryder snapped. "Cut through my saddle cinch, and then when it loosens the saddle and I'm trying to stay on my pony's back, you'll use your gun. You treacherous little basta—"

The words were never completed, as Ryder was forced to jerk his head swiftly to one side to evade the force of the thrown knife as it was hurled from Heffner's hand. He heard it hiss past his ear and slash against the front wall of Porky's saloon, even as his right hand swept down to holster.

Unbelievably fast as he was, Heffner's first shot missed, when Ryder threw his body to one side. Ryder released two flaming slugs of .44 lead, while Heffner was leveling his six-shooter for a second attempt. The shots echoed and re-echoed along the street. Heffner's second try had also missed, when the terrific impact of Ryder's bullets found their mark which almost lifted Heffner from his footing.

Ryder triggered a third shot from his gun muzzle, sending Heffner twisting convulsively to the earth, where he lay twitching like a rattlesnake in its death-throes.

There were sudden yells along the street and the sounds of running feet on board sidewalks. Ryder had just started toward his stricken enemy, when something struck his left shoulder a violent smash, hurling him half around and practically knocking him from his feet.

Dimly, he heard the resounding crack of a .30-30 Winchester, as he fought to regain his balance. It was a losing fight, but through a haze of black-powder smoke he made out Doag Barbe's red beard, across the street, as Barbe was levering a second cartridge into the rifle chamber.

Ryder was still staggering back, falling, when, with a supreme final effort, he sent a slug and jet of orange flame from his .44, in Barbe's direction.

And then, he could no longer maintain his balance, as he crashed to earth, on the way down striking his head a violent blow on the end-pole of the hitch-rail. An immense white explosion burst within Ryder's skull, blotting out all consciousness.

Chapter XVIII

Ryder awoke to find himself stretched in bed, with one shoulder swathed in bandages. He moved the arm a trifle. Well, it seemed to work all right, though a slight pain accompanied the movement. His gaze wandered around the room. The shade was half drawn. His eyes surveyed the room again. This wasn't his — and Sabina's — room. Who'd put him in the spare room? Why? Where was Sabina, anyway? Apparently, he'd been shot in the shoulder during the fracas. But who'd hit him? He was almost sure he had finished Burchard — Burchard? Something queer going on. Old memories, conflicting with new, flashed in and out of his mind. Well, he'd finish out his sleep. Things would come clearer, later, when he woke up again.

He heard a step in the room. Sabina was bending over him. He felt her warm lips on his own an instant. Then she straightened up, gazing searchingly into his eyes.

"You look like the old Dix, this morning," she laughed. "Have you come back at last, honey?"

He murmured sheepishly, "Have I been away long, darlin'?"

She said, "Five years."

He didn't get that. "What about Ross Burchard?" he asked.

"Burchard? Good grief, Dix, he died, five years ago."

There was that five-years-business again. His ears must be affected. "Well, how long have I been out?"

"About three weeks. You've been delirious, babbled incessantly. Sometimes you were in Texas, sometimes here."

"You hoorahing me," he asked skeptically. "I never spent much time in Texas — no, wait — yeah, I was in Texas. I don't remember what I did there. I'll think in a minute. My mind seems all cobwebby-like — can't think straight."

"Rest is what you need. Doctor Grissome says —"

"Who's Dr. Grissome? Whyn't you have old Doc Hartley?"

"Dr. Hartley died three years ago."

Ryder scowled. "I don't remember going to his funeral."

"You were in Texas."

"I was?" Ryder forced a wan smile. "I'm

sleepy. Let's save your riddles until I wake up."

"All right, I'll do that. I just wanted to say that Dr. Grissome says your shoulder is nearly mended. Said he couldn't understand why you remained out of your mind so long, so I told him what we'd been doing. Now, he says he understands — something happened to —"

"Who shot me?"

"It was right after you had to kill Vince Heffner, then Doag Barbe got into your fight, so Finch Orcutt says. You downed Barbe —"

"Heffner — Barbe? Never heard of 'em. What did they have against me? Wait, yes, those names are sorta familiar. Let me think."

"It'll all come clear after a while," Sabina said soothingly, "when you've had more rest. Charlie Tann has nearly driven me frantic. It seems he comes up to ask about every hour how you're getting along —"

"Tann? Charlie Tann. Is that somebody I should know? Damn! I'm more muddled than — yeah, Tann. I seem to remember I took a train ride with him once — lemme see, where did we go? I can't seem to recollect —" He tried to keep awake but he was getting more drowsy every minute. A moment more and he was sound asleep, breathing easily. Sabina tiptoed from the room.

She stood in the living room a minute, thinking, then left by the back door and, seeing Narcisso passing by, called to him and asked him to send Charlie Tann up to the house when he had a chance to come. She returned to the house, set out a bottle and glass on a table in the living room.

She had scarcely completed things when Charlie Tann arrived. She poured a drink of whisky and invited him to sit down. He took the whisky but didn't touch it at once. "Is — is Dix worse?"

"Better, Charlie."

Charlie looked relieved and sank into a chair, took a healthy swig of liquor and ejaculated, "That's mighty satisfactual — as Santone — er — Dix, used to say."

"Dix is correct, Charlie. I asked you to come up here to tell you a story. One day a man calling himself Santone Austin came here, after my husband, Dix Ryder, had vanished for five years. He was so like Dix that, after some explanations on my part, he agreed to stay here and pose as my husband —" From that point on, Sabina made Charlie familiar with the whole story, the difficulties she experienced on the DR and so on.

When she had concluded, Charlie's eyes bugged out. "You — you mean, Dix is *really* Dix Ryder? Good Lord, wait until I tell the rest of the boys — or perhaps I should keep silent — ?"

"Not at all, Charlie. I'll expect you to do just that. Just explain that his mind — his memory — might be a bit faulty at times, until he's entirely recovered. Dr. Grissome says he's had a form of amnesia due to some blow on the head, in the past, affecting him with a functional disturbance of memory. While he was delirious, the doctor and I both listened to his unconscious talk. At times he mentioned Texas days, and others he was back here. Certain events, people, were screened from his mind for a time."

"And you're sure he's really Dix Ryder?"

"There's no doubt in my mind. While I've been nursing him, I recognized an old scar across his ribs where a maddened cow's horn raked him one time. His mannerisms are the same. I roll cigarettes for him and sometimes smoke with him. Such things he takes for granted. And how many men do you find who use the word 'satisfactual,' so often? The one small doubt I had was when he said he had

246

owned the Monarch Ranch in Texas. Now, I knew that was an old outfit —"

"Good Lord, I can explain that Mrs. Ryder —"

"That's what I hoped you'd be able to do. From all I can pick up, you seem to be Dix's oldest friend. He's been vague on anything previous to the time of your acquaintance, and I've hesitated to push the subject too far. When did you first meet Dix? He said something about taking a train ride with you one time."

"That was the time," Charlie laughed, "though it's not so funny when I think back to those days. You see, I was just traveling through Arizona, on my way from California. Being slightly bereft of coin of the realm, those days, I'd decided to travel as the guest of the railroad company. The car I chose to occupy was one of a long string of empty box cars en route to the east. This particular freight vehicle fortunately had the door pushed back, so I climbed in and proceeded to make myself comfortable —"

"Good heavens! Comfortable in a box car?"

"One learns to adjust to circumstances," Charlie explained. "There was a heap of straw in one corner. I had a blanket and canteen of water, two thick sandwiches wrapped in newspapers. My pullman was a bit jolly at times, but I'd become accustomed to that sort of thing. There were various stops along the line, made to clear the way for passenger trains, while I was forced to await resumption of travel on a spur. One night we made a similar stop and were switched off to a spur down near a lot of cattle pens. I realize now that this particular stop was at Arboledo, though I didn't know the name of the town then —"

"And that is where Dix joined you?"

"Rather say, where he was forced to join me. At the time he knew nothing about it —"

"I remember that night." Sabina bit her lip. "Dix had ridden into town late to see the depot master in Arboledo — something about an extra shipment of cows he wanted to send off, and — and then — he never returned for five years."

"Anyway," Charlie resumed, "there I was sitting in the dark waiting for my car and the other freight cars to be jerked back on the main line again. The sky was full of stars, but there still wasn't much to be seen. I heard voices approaching and then footsteps. I gathered that the men were carrying something. I understood later they were carrying an unconscious Dix Ryder. Something was said about he'd never recover from the blow on the head with a chunk of scantling, as he emerged into darkness from the depot."

"That explains a lot," Sabina murmured.

"I shrunk back in a corner of the car and listened while the scoundrels planned to throw the body, as they put it, into the car with the open door that I was occupying. Then somebody else said something about wanting to make sure and I caught the explosion of a six-shooter. That raised a protest. The men feared the sound of the shot would rouse somebody else. Then a man started whining that the clothing would be bloody and he'd planned to change clothes. There was some arguing, and then a lot of talk about getting the togs off the stiff —"

"One of those men had changed clothing with Dix! He was the one, probably, that went to Mexico and was killed in a gun fight, when things were found in the pockets to identify the fellow with Dix. And he put his clothing on Dix —"

"Nope." Charlie Tann shook his head. "When they pushed Dix into the car he had only his underwear on — not even socks. About that time, I'd heard the train go through on the main line and our string of box cars jolted. In a short time we were under way again. So there I was, with a dead man, as I thought, for a traveling companion. Just before we pulled out, I heard the man who had taken Dix's clothing, cursing in a loud voice that the shot had ruined the cartridge belt —"

"I don't understand —"

"I didn't either, at the moment. I can only guess now that the man who'd fired at Dix, 'to make sure,' as he'd said, had struck Dix's cartridge belt, causing the bullet to glance off. That probably saved Dix's life, as his wound was really superficial — in the fleshy part over one hip — though it did bleed like the very devil. When I discovered he was still alive, I did what I could. With water from my canteen and a chunk torn from my shirt I accomplished a sort of bandaging job —"

"I noticed that old scar, when Dix was brought home," Sabina frowned. "I wondered, then, when —"

"Come morning — we must have been traveling across New Mexico — Dix regained consciousness. Though I'd finally got the bleeding stopped, he was pretty weak from loss of blood. Trouble was, he couldn't tell me who he was, didn't seem to remember anything. I explained what I had heard and asked where he was from. He didn't know — didn't even know his name. For a long time after that I just called him 'Pard.' We got off the train in the freight yards at El Paso —"

"Was Dix strong enough to walk?"

Charlie shook his head. "He had to be carried off. You see, a railroad detective discovered us, and promptly had Dix taken off to the hospital. He was a pretty decent fellow. He questioned me as to Dix's identity. I couldn't tell him anything. I was afraid to say too much, beyond the fact that some men had shoved Dix into my car, as I didn't know but that Dix had been in some sort of trouble. I guess the detective just put us down as a couple of hoboes, and forgot the matter, except that he had me arrested for vagrancy. I got thirty days in jail. When my sentence was up, they needed somebody to sweep out cells, deliver food to prisoners and so on. I got the job, so I was able to be on hand with some money when Dix was released from the hospital, though he was still very shaky."

"But how did you live?" Sabina asked.

"My job gave me enough money to rent a small shack and buy food until Dix was

251

stronger. All the time I was trying to get him to remember who he was, but he just shook his head in a dumb manner of speaking, as it were. I suspected he was covering up his past life, so I gave over questioning him —"

"But how did he acquire the Monarch Ranch?"

"I'm getting to that as fast as I can, Mrs. Ryder. The time came when Dix got restless, said he wanted to get out of El Paso. I could see something was bothering him, as though he realized he wasn't in the right place. Perhaps he thought traveling round might open the key to something. One night he borrowed ten dollars from me — that was the wages for my week — and got into a poker game. By the time we got home, he'd won two hundred dollars. That, he said, was our stake and that I'd brought him luck. He shucked the clothing the hospital had given him and bought cow puncher togs — that whittled our money down considerable. He even managed to get a cow pony — a crowbait, he termed it. That wasn't my idea of the way to travel, but I hated to turn him loose on his own. Somehow he managed to get a gentle mule for me to ride. I ache every time I think of following him around on that confounded mule. Here and there we'd get jobs at ranches. Somehow, I took a dislike to work, but I couldn't leave him —"

"You've been a real friend, Charlie."

Charlie scoffed at that. "We traveled from one end of western Texas to the other, never staying long in one place. His former life, which he never seemed to get back, receded farther and farther in the distance. He'd liked San Antonio when we were there, so I'd taken to calling him Santone. He seemed glad to adopt the name and said he should have another. I suggested Austin. From then on he was known as Santone Austin, wherever we went. Jobs came easy at various ranches. It was apparent he knew cows and horses and could handle a gun when necessary."

"Talking is dry work," Sabina suggested.

Charlie took the hint and poured himself a second glass of whisky. "Not so dry now," he smiled and went on, "Eventually, we landed at the Monarch Ranch and got jobs — I used to help around the kitchen. Dix liked the place and from things he dropped now and then I could see he felt himself a native Texan. He liked the Monarch crew. Now and then there were various skirmishes with cow thieves and Comanche Indians off the reservation, and

Dix always acquitted himself well. In two years he was appointed foreman of the ranch. Old Arch Montgomery had taken a liking to Dix and dumped most of the responsibility on Dix's shoulders. What Dix said, went, with Old Arch. Used to have Dix ride into town with him every weekend for the poker games at the hotel there. Dix always insisted I go along as his lucky piece."

Charlie paused to take a drink of whisky. "You know, they really play poker back in Texas. I've seen some pretty big games there, and mostly Dix came out a winner. And then one particular night there was a real tough game. There were Old Arch and three other ranch owners, all well-heeled, but Dix had the luck of the devil that night. He couldn't seem to lose. Hand after hand was played. Stopping only for a bite of food or a brief nap, the game continued the next day and the next and the next. I don't know much Dix had won by that time. The stakes were running extremely high, and I almost fainted at the size of some of the pots Dix gathered in."

"But I thought he'd owned the Monarch Ranch."

"He did. Old Arch Montgomery in an effort to retrieve his losses when he got a good hand, put up a half-interest in the ranch. One by one the other players had dropped out. There was only Dix and Old Arch left. Then the showdown came. Old Arch held four aces —"

"And Dix —"

"A royal flush!"

"Good grief! And Dix owned half a ranch. But what about Arch Montgomery? It seems hard luck to —"

"Not Old Arch. He took it all as a big joke on himself. Said he was glad to shift some more responsibility. Dix tried to persuade him to call off the whole deal, but Old Arch wouldn't hear of it. Said he'd wanted to retire for a long time and go to Denver where he had a married daughter — the only relation he had left. A few months later he offered to sell his half of the outfit to Dix on easy terms — claimed he was getting too old to handle cow problems."

"And Dix took him up on it?"

"Jumped at the chance, Mrs. Ryder. Then, later on, those oil millionaires showed up and made Dix a big offer for the Monarch. He jumped at it — been an idiot to refuse, sold the ranch, paid off old Arch Montgomery, and gave all his hands a big bonus. Then he announced he was going to do some traveling, west, as he'd never been in Arizona — so he said. I was going with him, but when I learned he was going to travel on horseback, I begged off. He'd promised to return, so most of his crew hung around town, waiting for him to come back — and then a telegram came to Matt Kimball, from here — well, you know the rest. I'm still wondering how he got shot up in Arboledo."

"I went to town," Sabina told him. "Talked to Finch Orcutt who had questioned every witness he could find. Vince Heffner attacked Dix, but Dix — er — finished Heffner. Then Doag Barbe fired at Dix, hit him in one shoulder. As he went down, Dix's single shot dropped Barbe. Dix must have struck his head against something as he dropped to earth, we don't know what. Anyway, Dr. Grissome said he had a lump there the size of a man's fist. The doctor thinks that that blow somehow restored Dix's thinking processes to order — that and the shock of the action, all at once."

"It sounds very possible," Tann agreed.

"As soon as Dix could be moved, the doctor had him moved here. Knowing that I'd had some medical training he realized I could nurse Dix better than anyone in

Arboledo. Once the bullet had been probed out of Dix's shoulder, the wound was really not serious. It was his mind that bothered us — and now that seems to be coming all right."

"That's good. Did Dix bring about Doag Barbe's demise too?"

"Barbe's being taken care of in town," Sabina said seriously. "He's unconscious — has been since Dix shot him. Dr. Grissome says there isn't a chance that he'd live and that only a bull-like constitution is keeping his heart beating."

They talked a while longer while Sabina got her mind cleared of a few more items that had puzzled her, then Charlie Tann returned to the bunkhouse to tell the story when the hands had returned from their day's range riding.

Chapter XIX

Dix had slept most of the day, so Sabina didn't rouse him to tell Charlie Tann's story. When she fed him that evening he mumbled something about things had begun to come clear in his mind, but that he felt rather confused. Thinking that sleep would do more toward restoring his strength than talk, she quickly departed from the room.

The following morning Sabina was aroused by a loud yell from the room where Dix was sleeping: "Sabina! Sabina, come here, quick!"

The girl hastily threw a wrapper about her slim form and hurried to the man's bedside. Dix was sitting up in bed, eyes wide. "Sabina," he exclaimed in some wonder, as she entered the room, "I'm Dix Ryder!"

"Of course you are, honey," she laughed.

"But I really am!" he insisted. "I've been thinking about things. A lot of incidents are dove-tailing that I've forgotten. You must believe me —"

"I never doubted you," the girl insisted. "Particularly when you were babbling so deliriously when you were only partly conscious. You said things that only you and I could know, about our former life, our wedding day — and — and — well, some of the things made me blush and the doctor had sense enough to leave the room —"

He grinned. "I'll have to learn to keep my big mouth shut. But I don't understand how I got to Texas."

"You just lie still and think while I get your breakfast. I talked to Charlie Tann yesterday and he cleared up a lot of things that had puzzled me."

Later, while she was feeding him from a tray, she told him what Charlie Tann had related. He nodded, "Yeah, I remember that train ride and getting to Texas — the hospital. And then us traveling around together. It was right rough going at times, but Charlie stuck to me like a cactus thorn in a bronc's saddle blanket. Y'know, I remember leaving here that night, five years back to go to the depot about an extra shipment of steers. I remember some rough looking scuts hangin' around the depot when I come out. Sure, Wickmann was among 'em — a different Wickmann from today. I remember being hit on the head from behind — serves me right for getting careless — and that's all. And then we were in Texas —"

"And it took another bullet wound and another wallop on the head to jolt you back where you belong — according to what the doctor says —"

"Sabina" — his eyes were wide — "this is the damndest thing! I've lived two lives. It's like I was watching a theatre play — it's not real. And I'm just watching a hombre called Santone Austin in all his scenes in Texas and then I see him riding here and meeting you — and — and —" He looked rather helpless. "By God, I've been watching myself play-acting my own life. It's, it's —" He floundered for the right words.

"Incredible," she supplied. "But good that it's true."

"Mighty satisfactual," he agreed. "Y'know, there was always a notion back in my head that something wasn't quite right. I felt I was a native Texan, when I was there, but dam'd if I could ever remember anything about a childhood. I got so I didn't even want to think about it, let alone talk of it to anybody. Say," — breaking off suddenly — "I know I got Heffner, but Barbe — ?"

"Barbe's still alive, but won't live the doctor says."

Dix shook his head. "That must have sure been one lucky shot. I remember fading and then, *wham!* Something put all my lights out." He ceased speaking and began to move about in bed.

Sabina frowned at him. "What do you think you're doing?"

"I'm going to get up," and at her protest, "why not? I'm Dix Ryder. I feel one hundred percent right —"

"You get back in that bed, Mr. Ryder," Sabina said sternly, "or you'll make no more lucky shots. I'd be almost willing to bet you your legs won't hold you upright. Now, get back there! You hear me?"

She pushed him back on the pillow and he grumbled something about coming home only to be henpecked — and almost instantly fell asleep again.

Two days later Dix was up and dressed for breakfast, legs still shaky, but less shaky as the day progressed. In three days he was back in the saddle for a short ride. In another three days he pronounced himself feeling as fit as ever, and he appeared so. More and more items were withdrawn from the pigeon-holes of his memory and cleared up. Now he was beginning to understand why Arboledo and many of the citizens, even Sabina, had seemed so familiar to him when he first arrived. The DR crew, amazed at his experience, was forced to laugh with him when he poked fun at himself and referred to himself as "Forgetful Ferdinand."

Nine days from the day he had first left his invalid's bed, he was seated at a table in the patio, slowly demolishing a cool bottle of beer and considering what his next move should be. The sun beat down through the boughs of the old cottonwood tree, dappling Ryder's form with black shadows. He lifted his head as he caught the sound of a horse loping past the house and down toward the corral. Within a few minutes, Marshal Finch Orcutt walked through the rear entrance of the patio, sombrero in hand, mopping his forehead with a damp bandanna.

At almost the same instant, Sabina hurried from the house, glass and bottle of beer in hand. "Saw you ride past the house," she commented. "Figured this might be welcome."

"You're an angel of mercy, Sabina," Orcutt laughed, sinking into a chair across the table from Ryder. "How's everything?"

"Never finer — now that Dix is back.

How are things in town?"

"Quiet — so far," Orcutt returned.

Ryder didn't miss the "so far," nor the look that passed across Orcutt's features. When Sabina had returned to the house he asked, "You certain Arboledo's quiet, Finch?"

Finch gave a short smile and wiped beer foam from his sweeping mustache. "Yeah, so far. I've had no trouble."

"Wickmann?"

"Not a word out of him. Nor, Hugo Ridge or 'Lonzo Tidwell — who seem to be Wickmann's close pals these days, since you downed Doag Barbe."

"What about Barbe? I'm told he's still unconscious."

"He died, early this morning, Dix."

Ryder's lips tightened. "God, I hate killing."

Finch said quietly, "Sometimes it's necessary, Dix. You know that as well as I do, if this country is ever to be settled peacefully. Arizona is no place for criminals. If you happen to be the instrument chosen by a higher power — oh, hell, you know what I mean. I just can't put it into words —" He broke off, changed the subject: "Speakin' truthfully, Dix, 'xactly how do you feel?"

Dix laughed and downed a swallow of beer. Orcutt followed suit. Dix said, "I'm as good as I ever was, Finch — better in some ways you might not understand until you get the whole story." Orcutt looked questioning, but Dix went on before he could start a query, "Did you have any particular reason to ask, Finch?"

Finch Orcutt nodded. "There's trouble coming, Dix."

Ryder said, level-voiced, "So?" And waited for an explanation.

"I sent a telegram to the sheriff at the county seat, this morning, stating there were storm clouds on the horizon, and asking to be made a deputy sheriff for this county."

"So?" Ryder said again. And again waited.

"Got an answer sooner than I expected, confirming my request, also giving me the authority to appoint any other deputy I might need. The telegram stated that a badge was being sent me by mail."

Ryder smiled. "I'd not expect the county seat to act so promptly."

Orcutt uttered a bitter laugh. "It's cheaper than sending a deputy here, Dix. So I am now a legally appointed deputy sheriff of Coyotero County in the sovereign Territory of Arizona —"

"Sounds impressive," Ryder laughed.

"And I'm now appointing you my assistant deputy. We won't bother with any of that swearing-in fooforaw. Anything I'll do — or you either — will be strictly legal —"

Ryder's lips twitched. "Do I get my badge by mail, too? Maybe I'd best buy some good polishing cream to keep my badge shined —"

"This is no laughing matter, Dix," Orcutt said seriously. "This country has been too long without a law man to overlook things. Now we've got proper authority — and we're going to need it. I've already appointed a feller in Arboledo to take over my marshalin' duties. Folks aren't so afraid to take some responsibility since you've returned and started in whittling down the bad element."

"Finch, what's back of all this business?"

"Doag Barbe died this morning —"

"So you said. I don't like to dwell on the thought. It was my bullet that —"

" 'Xactly. There was only Doc Grissome with him before he kicked the bucket. His mind was clear and he said he wanted to make a confession. I reckon he hated to face his Maker wearin' a blotted brand —"

"I'll be surprised if he ever gets to meet

his Maker," Dix interposed grimly.

"The Doc sent for me immediately. We were the only ones to hear the confession. Barbe pretty much cleared the boards for us. He told how Wickmann was back of all the skulduggery around here, and about his dirty deals. 'Course, we practically knew that, but we never had proof. After Barbe shuffled off, I went to Wickmann to see if he wanted to handle the funeral. Wickmann just laughed at me. I could see he was relieved that Barbe had passed on, but wanted to know if Barbe had talked about anything before he died. I told him Barbe hadn't. Also, following Sabina's suggestion, I didn't let on that you were well again. Grissome hasn't talked. Wickmann thinks that you're due to pass out at any minute. Then, with him thinking you're nearly dead, he can act."

"In what way?" Ryder asked, tight-lipped.

"Dix, do you know where Catamount Buttes is located?"

"Sure, but — what goes on there?"

Orcutt continued, "As I understand it, Catamount Buttes is situated in pretty rugged country —"

"Sure is. Haven't ridden in that direction for a coon's age — mebbe six or seven years — but I know 'em. Those buttes are located in up-and-down country, broken terrain, and so on. Not much good for grazing. On the other hand, there's a lot of trees grow over there, mesquite, palo verde, suharo cactus, and so on. Sure, I know that stretch; lies about five miles south of the DR boundary lines. What about it?"

"There's a box canyon over there, well grassed. That's where the Wickmann scuts held the DR cattle they stole from you, until they could change brands and resell the critters down below the Mexican border —"

"They got any of our beeves there now?" Ryder cut in.

Orcutt shook his head. "Not according to Doag Barbe. Matter-of-fact, Wickmann lost his nerve and turned some stolen steers back on DR holdings, before brands could be changed."

"That much I'd already suspicioned," Ryder nodded. "I'll give you the story later. What about Catamount Buttes?"

"There's a cave there, where Wickmann has a crew holed up, waitin' for orders, right near that box canyon. That cave is just below a queer formation in the rock, where a red streak slashes upward toward the top of a butte —"

"Hell, I remember seeing that place. There's a lot of tree growth around there. If there's a cave there I never saw it."

"There is," Orcutt stated grimly, "and all hell is due to break loose from that cave."

"In what way?"

"There's half a dozen or more cowhands living there. Now that Wickmann has the idea you're nigh dead, he's figuring to have those bastards raid the DR."

Ryder laughed. "They'll need more than a half dozen —"

"Not the way they'll work it," Orcutt said tersely. "While your outfit is asleep, one man will sneak in and lay dynamite in a couple of places against your bunkhouse. Once that is blowed up, where's your crew?"

Ryder's face clouded. "And then?"

"Then the scuts abduct Sabina and hold her in their cave until she consents to make over a bill-of-sale to Purdy Wickmann. If they find you still alive, they'll bump you off when they grab Sabina."

Ryder's voice was cold. "So we've got Wickmann cold turkey."

"How you figuring?"

"Barbe's confession. With evidence like that, no court would ever fail to convict Wickmann. Wickmann could be forced to return money he's made from his skulduggeries around here —"

"Not so fast, Dix. Remember, Doag Barbe is dead. Hearsay evidence won't stand up in court. Wickmann would deny everything — swear that Barbe was a liar. So there goes your case, shot to hell."

Ryder's face clouded. "I reckon you're right, Finch," he finally conceded gloomily.

"What you aimin' to do about it, Dix?"

Ryder didn't answer for a few moments. Then he said quietly, "I reckon we'll just have to be ready for the skunks when they arrive. Or, maybe we can forestall 'em. I've got to do some thinking on the subject. Thanks for warning me."

"*Por nada,*" Orcutt nodded. "For nothing. I had to let you know, that's all. Now, I've got to be back. Let me know what you intend to do, when you make up your mind, Dix. And remember, we've both got the law back of us now."

"I'm glad to have that authority. By the way, when is this raid on the DR supposed to take place?"

"Tomorrow night about midnight — when everybody's asleep," Orcutt replied. "According to Barbe, anyway."

Ryder gave a short laugh. "That soon?

I'll have to do some fast thinking, I reckon."

That night, at supper time, Ryder explained to his crew what Finch Orcutt had related. The men's faces went hard and taut while he talked.

"So we've got a good scrap on our hands, looks like," Malt Kimball said grim-featured.

Ryder nodded shortly. "Maybe so, maybe not. I've been thinking things over. I can't see any use of our gang getting knocked off. We'd be fools to wait here until they attacked. I figure we'd best carry the fight to 'em." He talked steadily for a few minutes, then concluded, "You hombres had better roll into blankets right after you finish eating. I figure we'd better leave here a mite before midnight. Just make sure your irons are well oiled and you have plenty ca'tridges. Jeff Clayton's got a supply of Winchesters here. Better figure to carry long guns too. Could be, you'll need 'em."

After he had left the bunkhouse, the crew finished its supper and then concentrated on the business of getting firearms in efficient shape, which of course hadn't been actually necessary.

Over supper with Sabina, Dix said carelessly, "By the way, I'll be sleeping down in the bunkhouse, later tonight." When she asked the reason, looking somewhat disappointed, he explained. "There's some stuff along the south DR boundary line — and beyond that — I want to get cleared up. We'll be leaving early, before daylight. No use awaking you when I leave."

Sabina misunderstood his allusion to "stuff." She nodded, saying, "It seems as though you'll never finish gathering in all our stock, Dix."

Dix laughed genially. "Seems that way, doesn't it? But, Sabina, darlin', I figure we're just about cleaned up. And then — and then, you and I can look forward to a lot of peaceful days. How's that sound?"

"I don't think," the girl smiled, "I've heard anything better. Here, let me pour you another cup of coffee and then roll your cigarette."

Chapter XX

Shortly before midnight, that night, Ryder led his mounted crew away from the DR Ranch and headed south. The men rode easily in a leisurely lope beneath the star-sprinkled sky, facing into the soft breeze lifting from the south bringing with it the scent of sage. Half way to Catamount Buttes he gathered the riders around him and explained his plan, concluding, "I know the spot. Unless it has changed a heap, there'll be plenty of trees and brush for concealment. How's the idea sound to you?"

Immediately there arose a chorus of protests. Ryder raised one hand. "Now, wait a sec. I figured this out as the only way to draw those scuts into the open, where you can surround them, instead of staging a long senseless business of exchanging shots."

"It's too risky for you, Dix," Jeff Clayton stated flatly. The other men staged similar objections, Matt Kimball interposing, "Jeff is right, Dix —"

"You're crazy as hell, Matt," Ryder

snapped, "and if you'll recollect we pulled something like this back in Texas, three years ago."

Reluctantly, Kimball conceded Ryder was right. "But you was lucky that time. You can't count on luck twice —"

"Why can't I?" Ryder interrupted.

That, Kimball couldn't answer. "I still don't like it," he grumbled. "They could get you."

"Not so long as I'm alert!" Ryder said. The men still voiced their protests. Impatiently, Ryder said, "Who's giving the orders around here?"

"You are, of course," Kimball replied promptly. "But —"

"But me no buts," Ryder stated caustically. "This is the way we are going to do it, whether you hombres agree or not. Good God, what are you trying to do, make heroes of yourselves? Do you prefer some of you get rubbed out in open battle? Hell's bells on a tomcat! You talk like a bunch of dumb cow-nurses, which same you're not. You're DR riders. So it's settled then. Let's push on. I want to arrive just about the time those scuts are starting breakfast — when they're not thoroughly awake. I want to catch 'em by surprise."

He didn't await further conversation, but

gave the word to ride on. They pushed through the starry night, the country becoming more rugged as they progressed.

Gradually, the way became less rolling, grass country and plain flattened out as they neared the vicinity of Catamount Buttes, a series of abruptly rising sandstone cliffs, lifting from the plain below — cliffs that were slashed and jagged from centuries of rain and wind, something foreboding in their grim majesty as they rose precipitatively toward the heavens. Now the way was gravelly beneath the horses' hoofs; there was much broken rock scattered about, and the riders moved slowly lest their mounts' hoofs made any noise.

It shouldn't have been any place for vegetation, but the section near the buttes was thick with brush, high mesquite, burgeoning clumps of tall prickly pear cactus and saltbush and catclaw.

A gray streak appeared in the eastern horizon, changed to red and then orange and yellow. Overhead the few drifting clouds were painted on the undersides with crimson. Growth began to take form and reveal details not to be seen a half hour before. Gradually a gray light spread over the range and began to show undertones of pink. The jagged buttes stood out clearly now, their edges etched sharply into view.

By the time full daylight had arrived, every man of the DR crew sat his horse behind the shelter of a tall mesquite or towering rise of prickly pear, completely concealed from the view of any hostile watcher, hard-faced and with hand always in the vicinity of his Colt's gun or Winchester trigger.

Screened by the branches of a big cottonwood tree, Ryder sat his saddle next to Jeff Clayton's horse, gaze swiftly surveying the face of the buttes, seeking the first glimpse of the enemy. It was broad daylight by this time. Finally Dix spied the red slash in a cliff.

Then, in a rift in the butte face, Ryder found what he sought. "There!" he spoke in a whisper to Clayton. "See it, Jeff?"

A thin column of blue smoke was rising from a spot screened by low brush and behind the smoke was to be seen a deep declivity in the rock face of the butte.

"That's the cave," Clayton nodded, "the hideout —"

"I'd best get started," Ryder stated shortly. "You all know what to do. Close in at the first shot."

"Don't worry. We'll take care of it,"

Clayton nodded. "Watch yourself, Dix!"

"The same to you," Ryder laughed shortly. "If my plan works, we'll have no worries, Jeff. S'long."

He spoke to his horse, lifted his reins, then rode into full view of anyone who might care to see, in the direction of the cave mouth, the early morning sun already beating down hard on his sombreroed head and casting a black shadow across the earth as he moved at a leisurely lope, eyes on the line of smoke rising from behind the brush.

He was less than a hundred yards from the cave mouth when he raised his voice: "Hullo, the camp!"

For a moment there was no reply as the call echoed and re-echoed across the plain. Then there was movement in the brush before the cave and he caught the sound of Alonzo Tidwell's voice: "By Gawd! It's Dix Ryder — all alone — !"

And another voice, "Get the son of — !"

Ryder didn't wait to hear more. There were wild yells, as he tossed the horse's reins over its head and threw himself to earth an instant before a flash of white fire spurted from the brush and the crack of a gun was heard to split the atmosphere.

"Got him!" somebody yelled.

Ryder lay motionless on one side, eyes peering at the group of men who came rushing from the cave mouth, guns ready for further shots. His horse had trotted a few yards away and then come to a stop.

There was another shot and sand spurted into Ryder's face.

Then there came a series of shots, and wild yells, as the DR riders left their concealment and plunged into the open. Bewildered, the Wickmann gang halted, then two of them started at a run back toward the cave, bullets kicking up dust as they moved. One uttered an agonized cry and went sprawling to the earth. The other stopped abruptly and raised his arms in the air in token of surrender.

There came a ragged volley from the other men who had started toward Dix, then they scattered in sudden confusion, suddenly uttering cries of surrender. One didn't speak soon enough, and he went down as though his legs had been swept away beneath him.

By this time Ryder was on his feet, six-shooter in hand, then he shoved the weapon back in holster as the horses of his men closed in around the abject outlaws who were huddled together looking very frightened.

The dust settled, while the Wickmann men were being disarmed. Of the two that had fled toward the cave, one was dead. Two more were groaning over wounds that would soon heal. Dix ran his eyes rapidly over his crew of riders "Anybody get hit?"

Nobody had. "That," Dix grinned, "is the way I like to do business. The surprise was complete. Now you can take 'em into town. They sound like they're ready to do some talking." He caught sight of Jeff Clayton nearby. "It worked, didn't it?" he laughed.

"Yes, you utter damn' fool," Clayton agreed. He still looked shaky from the risk that Ryder had taken. "Now you can fire me for talking back —"

"Fire you hell!" Ryder laughed. "I need you too much. While I'm gone you can round up these scuts' horses and bring 'em to town. They're all under arrest, of course. Turn 'em over to Marshal — er — Deputy Sheriff Orcutt."

"Where you going?" Clayton asked.

"Arboledo. I figure, personally, to put Wickmann under arrest —" He broke off, striding across the earth where his horse patiently awaited him. He paused a moment as he climbed into the saddle and turned the horse toward town. "I'll see you

278

all later, hombres!"

Matt Kimball yelled after him, "Wait, Dix, mebbe some of us better go with you."

But Ryder was already spurring into motion, hurling his mount in great leaps in the direction of Arboledo.

It was something under ten-thirty when Ryder jerked his lathered horse to a stop at the hitch-rack in front of the building where Purdy Wickmann had his quarters. He paused a moment on the sidewalk, glancing both ways. The sun beat down hotly on one side; the other side was in black shadow. Only a few people were to be seen on the sidewalks, and not very many wagons and ponies lined the hitch-racks. Later, when the heat of the day passed, the town would show more activity. At the moment, a sort of somnolence hung over Arboledo.

Ryder nodded to a man who passed and continued to study the building, where a flight of stairs led up the outside wall to Wickmann's quarters.

"Wonder if he's up there," Ryder mused. "Perhaps, I should leave this attesting to Finch Orcutt." Then, coming to a sudden decision, "No, by God, this is between Wickmann and me. This is my job."

He started forward. His hand was steady on the scantling handrail as he mounted the steps. On the landing at the top, he paused a moment, leaning against the railing while he surveyed the street below, then switched his gaze to the closed door facing him. He told himself, again, "This is my job."

Doubling his fist, he knocked sharply on the door. Instantly, came Wickmann's voice, "Who's there?"

"Dix Ryder."

There came the sound of an oath from within, then Wickmann again, "Go 'way. I'm busy. No time to talk to you now."

"Better open up, Wickmann. I'm putting you under arrest."

No reply this time, except for a low cursing. Ryder raised his voice again, "Your game's finished, Wickmann," Ryder called. "We raided the hideout in Catamount Buttes. You might as well surrender peacefully."

Still no reply from within the room. And now, Ryder mused grimly, he's trying to decide whether to give up, or use that under-arm gun he totes. Well, we'll see.

He tried the door knob. It turned but the door refused to open. It was locked. Dix called, "You'd best open up, Wickmann.

One way or the other, I'm coming in."

Wickmann didn't reply.

Ryder raised one booted foot, jammed it hard against the closed door. There came the sound of splintered wood, but the door held. Ryder backed off a step, braced himself against the railing at his back, then with a rush threw his shoulder into the door. This time the lock shattered, the door swung partly ajar. Ryder raised his foot again, slamming into the partly opened door. It swung violently back, two swift slugs, followed by thundering reports, flashing through the open doorway.

But Ryder had been prepared for that, as he crouched low, firing from the vicinity of his hip as he leaped within the room. The force of the heavy .44 bullet swung Wickmann back against the far wall, as another shot thudded into the wall near Dix's shoulder. Instantly he shifted his gaze and saw Hugo Ridge backed to the far side of the room, teeth bared in a savage snarl, just lifting his gun for another shot.

Ryder was moving too fast to make a good target and Ridge's shot missed. Ryder felt the .44 leap in his hand. Orange flame ran from the muzzle to end in a puff of dust on Ridge's vest.

Ridge was swept to one side by the force

of the blow, knocking into Wickmann and spoiling the man's next shot. Instantly, as Wickmann staggered to one side, Ryder fired again. And again.

Eyes wide with horror, Wickmann tried to escape through the open doorway, booted feet moving fast to regain his balance, carrying him in a staggering run outside where he struck the handrail with a smashing thud. The wooden railing held but a moment, then there came a sharp shriek of breaking wood. The railing gave way, and Wickmann plunged heavily to the earth below.

Startled yells were heard from the street. Running feet pounded along the sidewalks. Ryder went to the broken stair railing, glancing down. Wickmann lay there, motionless, like an old heap of castoff clothing. Ryder returned to the room. Heavy clouds of powdersmoke hovered near the ceiling. The odor of burnt powder stung eyes and throat and nostrils. Ryder's gaze sought Hugo Ridge. The body of the man lay huddled against the foot of Wickmann's desk. There wasn't any movement there, either.

Dix said tiredly, half-aloud, "He looks dead."

There were clumping steps on the

stairway. Finch Orcutt entered the room. "My God, what's happened?"

Ryder said in weary tones, "We raided that cave in Catamount Buttes this morning. My crew will be bringing you some prisoners shortly. Then I came here, figuring to put Wickmann under arrest. You can see what happened, though I didn't know Ridge was with him."

"Gawd," Orcutt said, "you were fast to get 'em both."

"I was fast enough." Ryder nodded, starting to reload his six-shooter.

"I sent a man for Doc Grissome the instant I heard the shots," Orcutt was saying.

Ryder waited until the doctor had arrived. He examined Wickmann then mounted the stairs, shaking his head. He pronounced Ridge dead, adding, "Some life left in Wickmann, but he won't last long. Says he wants to do some confessing."

Ryder turned away. "We can settle matters tomorrow, Finch. Anything legal to be settled, I'll be here. I'm leaving."

"Where you going?" Orcutt asked.

"Home — home to Sabina," Ryder explained quietly.

He walked slowly down the stairway,

pushed his way through the crowd of curious onlookers and climbed into the saddle.

Once more he had his horse turned toward home. . . .

We hope you have enjoyed this Large Print book. Other Thorndike Press or Chivers Press Large Print books are available at your library or directly from the publishers.

For more information about current and upcoming titles, please call or write, without obligation, to:

Thorndike Press
P.O. Box 159
Thorndike, Maine 04986 USA
Tel. (800) 257-5157

OR

Chivers Press Limited
Windsor Bridge Road
Bath BA2 3AX
England
Tel. (0225) 335336

All our Large Print titles are designed for easy reading, and all our books are made to last.